Joshua Ra

5fingers: freedom into the light

5fingers book five

°°°°°*12345*°°°°°

Moja, mbili, tatu, nne, tano,
nimepata samaki, mkubwa mno.
Nawe mwenye nguvu,
kwanini ukamuwachia?
Kaniuma kidole.
Nalia eee, eee.

°°°°°*12345*°°°°°

Red Ink. Publishing

Also by Joshua Raven

Joshua Raven – 5fingers: freedom

Follow Joshua Raven's blog at www.joshuaraven.com

Instagram: @RavenWrites

Twitter: @RavenWrites

Facebook: Joshua Raven Author

Pinterest: Joshua Raven 5fingers

Joshua Raven – 5fingers: freedom
Copyright © Arif A Mohamed, 2018

Published by Red Ink Publishing Limited
All rights reserved Red Ink Publishing Limited
Arif A Mohamed has asserted his rights under the Copyright,
Designs and Patents Act, 1988 to be identified as the author of
this work

www.5fingers.co.uk
www.redinkpublishing.co.uk

Production by JAC Design, Clockhouse Court, Beacon Road,
Crowborough, East Sussex TN6 1AF

Cover design and artwork by Lewis Design

ISBN 978-0-9934011-6-9

Printed and bound in Great Britain by TJ International Ltd.

This novel is dedicated to Phoebe, the love of my life, my fellow adventurer and best friend.

A huge thank you to my most excellent 5fingers fans who make all this worthwhile; my wonderfully-supportive family, and my editors: Phoebe, Rebekah, Joshua, Caleb, Jo, Mark and Kate. To Louis at Lewis Design, Carole and Jane at JAC Design, Neil at Copytech, and Jane at JG Accounting – you are all rock stars and I am grateful to you all.

To all the dead giants who've made my writing come alive – I stand on your shoulders. Franz Kafka, Charlotte Bronte, Stanislaw Lem, C.S. Lewis, Charles Dickens, Philip K. Dick, John Milton, Fred Pohl, John Webster, Fyodor, Dostoevsky, T.S. Eliot, Jane Austen, J.R.R. Tolkien, Roald Dahl, William Shakespeare, Emily Bronte, Alfred Bester, Virginia Woolf, Geoffrey Chaucer, Agatha Christie, Henry James, Daniel Defoe, Leo Tolstoy, James Joyce, George Eliot, John Bunyan, Jonathan Swift, Laurence Sterne, Flann O'Brien, Marion Zimmer Bradley, Aleksandr Solzhenitsyn.

Chapter 1

The earth cowered in the darkness. Half of it was steeped in black night. The other smothered in smoke and smog. Plumes of demons spiralled through space. They tangled with angels of light, battling relentlessly. It was a timeless dance. A treacherous clash. A fight to the death. The prize was a priceless pearl: the eternal soul of slumbering humanity.

A lone figure walked the land, sending out a white glow wherever he went. He looked kindly on Rachel Race in her cell. Stroking her hair as she slept. He also visited Iona in the night. And Lara across the Atlantic in Laguna Bay, California. She sat in a chair: lost in thought. Remembering home with a heavy heart. He sang a tune over her then moved quietly on.

The traveller wandered through Lytescote Manor. He was free to go wherever he chose, because the world was his. But Samyaza, the enemy, growled as he passed by. The demon lord knew his time on earth was short. Time was running out. There was much work to do. He spat at the man as he passed by, and slid through the wall like a ghost.

The Dream Fighters abandoned Kumiko on the cold driveway. Their former leader. Their "master". And that was where he found her. Discarded. Alone. The outdoor lights laid bare her slender form. Her long arms and legs poking out of a slim black dress.

"You know who I am, don't you," he said. It was a statement, not a question.

She stared sadly at him from the hard ground where she lay. Her bones ached. Samyaza had thrown her, like a ragdoll, at the wall. It was all she could do to crawl out through the front door and collapse. She had given up on her broken body. Everything hurt. She wanted to die.

"Go away," she groaned.

Yes, she knew who this man was. Instinctively. She glanced up at him. He wore a platinum band around his head. A waterfall of long white hair fell over his shoulders. His face glowed against the night sky. A luminous moon on a nursery ceiling. He was the Rescuer. Her sworn enemy.

He knelt down. She felt his hands on her side. They rested there for a while. Moments later, her pain evaporated. Three broken ribs became whole. He passed his fingers over her arm and healed her broken shoulder and busted forearm.

Reading her thoughts he said, "Yes, I am. And I love you, Kumiko Starkweather. I love you with a fierce passion. And from now on you are Kumiko Fairweather."

"Huh. Like fair-weather friend?" she muttered.

"No. Like the fair weather of a warm summer's day," he answered gently. "You are a fresh breeze. An evening whisper. I love the summer evenings with their long hours of light and hope. And I love you."

"How can you love me? I hate you. You and your people. I wanted to destroy it all." But, as she said the words, it felt as though she was trying to remember somebody else's thoughts. Someone else's agenda. Her eyes were wet with tears. Her mind grey with confusion.

"I hated you," she muttered. But she looked at his face in the moonlight and it was beautiful and kind. He gazed at her with love and concern. Focused his full attention on her alone and there was no malice in his eyes. So unlike Samyaza who had cruelly betrayed her. Samyaza the deceiver.

Did she really hate the Rescuer King? The pain left her legs. They buzzed with warmth. How had she been so taken in by

8

Samyaza? So blinded by his lies? Strength returned to her body and she sat up slowly.

All around her were figures. Bulky, black-winged beings. Some of them hovered above the ground. Leather-clad Dream Fighters stood at their stations, dressed in their black and brown tunics. But nobody approached her. They left her alone.

"Wait here," said the Rescuer. "Rest a moment. I have made you safe. No harm will come to you from now." He began to walk towards the door of the mansion.

"Don't leave me," she pleaded.

"I won't be long."

Inside, he went to Daniel Harcourt's office where Samyaza, the Grigori, was still in residence. His hideous face was cast down to the ground as his visitor entered. But Samyaza jerked his head up and snarled as he approached.

The Rescuer spoke in melodious tones with authority. "You have oppressed my people. There is a price to be paid." He stood tall, eyeing the enemy fiercely from beneath his white hair.

Samyaza opened his mouth to speak. Rotten, raisin-black teeth jutted out from his cavernous maw.

"Be silent," commanded the Rescuer. "I do not permit you to speak yet. Only listen. You have a choice. You always have a choice. I will ask you once again. Will you stop? Now you may speak."

Samyaza gritted his teeth and stared balefully through two milky orbs.

"So be it," said the King. "The day of your judgement will be severe." He turned on his heel and strode back to rescue Kumiko.

Chapter 2

Rachel's Diary

Day 1. I need to get this down. Not that I think anyone's going to read it. This notepaper and a pen were on the shelf in my room. My cell.

It's been a really long day but I want to get this down. I need to, for my own sanity. I think they're going to kill me. I don't know when. Maybe tomorrow. Maybe they'll keep me alive like he said. That horrible monster.

Samyaza.

I don't know what they'll do to me. I keep trying to push it out of my mind. Out of my mind. Maybe I am out of my mind.

But let me start from the beginning because I'm getting random, as I always do. I'm Rachel Race. I'm seventeen. And I'm scared.

This could be the last thing I ever write. There's a knife on the table. The handle's jade green. I don't want to think about it. I can use it on myself any time I want to, he said. But I don't want to. I really don't. It's got a big jagged edge, with serrated teeth like a handsaw. I hate the look of it. I haven't touched it. I left it on the table.

They haven't hurt me yet. Apart from when the men took me. I've got a bunk to sleep on. I also have a wooden chair. And there's the shelf with the notepaper and pen on it. But I mentioned that already, didn't I? There's a toilet in the corner. But I'm getting random again. Lara always used to tell me off for being too random. But she was quite random as well, so that's pretty rich coming from her. I guess it's why we like each other. I wonder how she is. I miss her. I miss Iona too. And Lake. I miss Lake a lot. But I should start from when they captured me.

I was in the mountains with Lake and Dad. That was when they grabbed me. We came out of the stone head. We'd gone across the mezzanine. The place where the sky is crazy purple. I faced all those horrible demons. Then the angels saved us. It was totally amazing. And when we got through, it was freezing cold in the mountains. Dad spotted a tent. They went to have a look. Only I got taken. There were two men. Big men. I didn't see their faces. One of them picked me up. He put me over his shoulder. He was too strong for me. When I tried to get free, he hit me. So I played dead. I was terrified. My head was throbbing.

They carried me for a long time, taking turns. I was like a sack of potatoes. They never got tired. Just kept going. Like they were on steroids or something. Or Terminators. Whenever I opened my eyes to look around, all I could see was snow. It all looked the same. White. Like a ghost world. There was nowhere to escape even if I could. I called on the Rescuer all the time. He didn't save me. I couldn't hear the voice of the Dunamis. I couldn't even feel him inside me.

It was like my heart was dead.

I just read all that back to myself. My English teacher, Mrs Baker, she'd be so proud of me. I always liked writing. Even though this is such a hard story to tell. Because it's real life.

So anyway, they stuck me in a metal box. It was just big enough to get up and walk around. It stank: rusty and stale. The box had some round holes at the top. There was just enough light to see. They gave me some food. A crust of bread. Some water. They even let me go to the loo. It was so kind, like really. They kept me blindfolded for that, but took it off when they put me back in the cage. I was their prisoner. Still am.

I fell asleep for a long time. I think it was a long time. I was

11

so tired. When I woke up, I was all alone in this room. There's one light, high up on the wall. Too high for me to reach. I'm not that tall, you know. It's a lemon-yellow oval with two thin metal strips that hold it in. The door is made of metal too. The walls are whitewashed and smell of paint. I've got no windows.

I took my bed apart to check there wasn't anything under the mattress. I don't know what I expected to find. It's just a plain mattress with a thick coffee-brown blanket. There are no trapdoors or any other ways to get out. Shame.

I could grab the knife and use it against them. But that's the other thing. I don't think it would work against him. The monster.

They left me for a long time, alone with my thoughts. I kept listening out for sounds, but it was quiet out there. Those hours were horrendous. I was too scared to be hungry. I did use the toilet once though. I tried to be really quiet so they didn't come in. I washed my hands with the little bar of soap. But there was nothing to dry them on. So I shook them for a while. Then I sat on the bed again.

After absolutely ages, the door opened. I jumped. And then I saw him. I knew straightaway it was him. His face was the thing that got me. It's hard to describe. It was so horrible. His face was like a skull. Cream and ebony-coloured. I could see his teeth and they were rotten. It was hard to look at him. His eyes are... They're dead. Full of hate. Like that shape-shifter, Zed.

He came in and stood there, not saying anything. His body was dark, kind of like those creatures in the mezzanine. And he had wings that came out of his shoulders. His teeth were sharp. I sat frozen on the bed. Gagging on the stench of rotten meat. I thought he was going to kill me there and then. But he didn't.

My mind went blank. Like the sand on Griffton beach when the sea has just gone out. It felt like I was being washed by heavy waves. Waves of fear. Waves of despair. I don't know. I felt completely alone. Exposed. I was defenceless in the presence of evil itself. And then he spoke.

"Rachel Race. We meet at last, face to face." The sound of his voice grated in my ears. His words were hollow and mocking. He moved in a weird way. It wasn't human. Sometimes his head would turn too fast. Or his wings would jerk like a squirrel darting up a tree.

He carried on in a low growl. "The last time you met me, you might remember, we ate together? I was in the body of Benson Steel. That loathsome creature thought the world owed him everything. I murdered him, you know. Made him jump out of a window. From his own offices. Served him right. He let me down. He failed to kill you. And I'm patient, very patient. But we will come to that in due course."

As he spoke, it was like I was watching one of those animated dinosaurs in a museum. I think they call it Animatronics. I could see his jaw moving and words coming out. But it wasn't like it was real. Except I knew it was. I glanced up at him. He looked like he had the power to kill me in an instant. Snap my neck like a plastic teaspoon.

He got louder. "I hate you Rachel Race. You represent each and every snivelling child who's ever put their faith in a rescuer and the lie of eternal life. I hate you because you're gullible, easily brainwashed by the propaganda of controlling people. About a Creator who cares about you. More fool you. There is no Creator any more than there are fairies at the end of the garden. There is only pain and death. And in between, there is a whole heap of bad luck and tiny, little, hollow victories. And then there's me. I am the ultimate reality and this world is mine."

He was looking around the cell as he spoke, but stared at me all of a sudden. It made me jump.

"You can still join me, you know. You still have time. A bit of time. You just have to say the words: "I will follow you." Do you want to say it now and save yourself a lot of pain?"

I was speechless and my heart was thumping. I closed my eyes to block him out.

"No? That's okay. I am going to keep you alive for seven days. And in that time, I will convince you that you are completely

13

alone and helpless in this universe. I'm going to keep you alive for seven days and then I am going to kill you. Unless you pick up the knife before then. Or say those four little words. "I will follow you." It's your choice. I always give humans a choice."

I kept my eyes shut for a very long time.

When I opened them, he wasn't there anymore.

Chapter 3

After he left the room, I stayed sitting on my bed for a long time. I stared at the metal door of my cell. I was scared he'd open it and come in, but glad he was on the other side.

My mind was racing. I had just seen the most evil thing on the planet. A being so nasty and full of hatred. So menacing. I was in his presence. It was horrible to think about. But he hadn't killed me. So, what does that mean? Does it mean he can't? Am I protected somehow? Or are they going to hurt me? Drive me to kill myself to avoid the beatings? So many questions. I don't want to think about them but I can't stop myself.

After a while, I got this horrible feeling I was being watched. I was convinced there were cameras everywhere. In the walls. These whitewashed walls. Or in the light fitting. Embedded in there. No, this is crazy, I thought. So, I looked hard at every crack in the wall. Anything that looked like a hole. I didn't find anything though. In the end, I came to the conclusion that if they are watching me, then so what? There isn't anything I can do about it. I don't have anything to hide.

I caught myself fiddling with the pockets of my combat trousers. I'm still wearing the outfit I had on in the mountains of Bhutan, you know. It was so cold there. My face froze. This cell, on the other hand, is warm in comparison, despite the metal, and the cold, smooth floor.

I stood up, removed my body warmer and threw it on the bed. I had my long-sleeved T-shirt underneath. My hair was dirty. I needed a wash. Pacing up and down the little room, memories came thick and fast.

I pictured Dad, but not like he was before, all grumpy and mean. I saw him with white hair and a big smile for me. Like he was after he met the King and got transformed by him. What was it Samyaza called me? Gullible and easily brainwashed? No. He's wrong. I know deep down that I've met the Rescuer. And Dad met him too. And Daniel and his family. And Caleb. I didn't make it up. I didn't dream it. It really happened. He did something to me. Liquid fire. He poured liquid fire into me and changed me forever. I've been cut from fire. Made into something new. That old emotional wreck of a girl, that Rachel the drama queen, she's gone. Long gone.

I remembered the Warrior Angels rescuing me from the black creatures in the mezzanine. Teeth and claws and wings. They were going to kill me. No question. Tear me apart. Dad and Lake were next.

But something in me told me to trust. Surrender to the Rescuer and trust him. And so I did. The old Rachel would never have done that. No, she would have worried herself into a coma. But the King changed me and gave me a glimpse of life beyond. The life beyond this one. The one that goes on forever. This life is the illusion. The one that lasts a second. The other one? Well, that's something else completely.

So, he's wrong. Samyaza is wrong. And I will not follow him. Not now, not ever. He can do what he wants to me. But I hope he doesn't hurt me.

I climbed onto the bed. Lying there, staring at the white ceiling. I'd had enough and wanted to go home. The bright light at the top of the wall shone cruelly. Like a bully who never went away.

"Rescuer, help me," I pleaded quietly, only nothing happened. I couldn't feel the Dunamis: the presence of the King with me - inside me. Even though he promised he'd never leave me, he'd always be with me. Despite that, it felt like he'd abandoned me. I looked up and saw the ceiling high above me.

"Where are you?"

I was talking to myself. It was pointless. I shut my eyes.

Just then, the metal door swung open. It made me jump. I stared across the room, my heart in a knot. It wasn't him. It wasn't Samyaza. It was a boy. One of the guards.

He was around my height and slim, holding a tray of food with both hands. Small hands. It was all incredibly normal, but at the same time very strange, now I come to write about it. I was their prisoner. I only ate if and when they let me. Someone outside pulled the door closed behind him.

I sat up on the bed, drew my legs together and hugged them to my body. I stared at him through my hair: a curtain of white strands.

He was a Dream Fighter. They wore leather outfits with a sash across their middles. This one wore a chocolate-brown cap on his head. His boots were muddy.

I'd seen them before. The first time was on Griffton Cliff when I went into that portal. The stone head. I was with the Harcourt family. The Dream Fighters chased us that night. Next time, I saw them in Griffton. And they took over Daniel's house. So, does that mean I am in Daniel's house? Is the mud on the soldiers' boots from outside the mansion?

The boy interrupted my train of thoughts. "So, you're the troublemaker?" he asked, sneering.

I kept silent.

"I have some grub for you. Hungry?"

I nodded. The boy moved closer and I moved back. The last thing I wanted was for him to play nice and then try and touch me or something.

He stopped in his tracks, pausing right in front of me. I noticed his face was smooth and clear. Clean-shaven. He had sharp, lively eyes. Cornflower blue.

"I'm not here to hurt you. In fact, Samyaza wants you to know he is not an animal." Despite delivering this line, I noticed my jailer seemed to shiver when he said the name of that horrible monster.

I raised my eyebrows.

"He says that, for the time being, he's happy for you to eat. You can even take a shower later, if you like." He raised his eyebrows as he said 'shower' and I glanced away to avoid his eyes.

Then he added, "I might even be allowed to take you for a walk down the corridor as well. But not very far. Just to stretch your legs. That's what they said."

"Lucky me," I said under my breath.

"Look, I'm going to level with you." He crept over and plonked the tray down at the end of my bed. I didn't look to see what was on it. I guess I was trying to use the small scrap of control I had.

He continued in hushed tones, but spoke fast, saying, as far as I remember: "This really isn't what I signed up for. That's all I can say. You should know you're not their only priority. There's a lot going on out there. In the city and across the world. And don't worry. They're not watching you. There's no cameras. It's just that they'd rather you were in here than out there. It's better for them."

It was like he was reading my mind.

"I'm really not here to hurt you," the guard said. "I used to be a finance assistant in the city, you know. I was in one of the big accountancy firms in Griffton. I had a normal life. This isn't what I wanted to do. The problem is I don't have a choice and that's all I can say."

I was surprised at his openness. And then he took his cap off. Long corn-yellow hair tumbled out. It was quite a party piece.

"I'm Sam by the way. Samantha." She held out her hand. I stared at it, in shock. After a while, she pulled her hand back.

Chapter 4

My jailer was a girl, not a young man. Once my brain caught up, I found myself relaxing. It was like a huge weight lifted off my chest.

Of course, she could still be dangerous. But she didn't really look it. If it came down to it, I reckon I could win in a fight.

"You're a girl," I said stupidly.

"Oh, sorry. I thought you knew that. Oh, you thought I was being friendly because… Oh, no. Like I say, Rachel, I'm doing this because I have to, not because I want to. But you need to promise me you won't tell anyone out there that I'm not one hundred percent Dream Fighter."

"Okay."

"And I'll do what I can for you."

"It's a deal," I said.

"Good. But I can't get you out of here. And don't ask me any questions. Understood?"

"Understood."

"And don't make my life difficult. Then, maybe, you and I can be friends." She looked at me with her round blue eyes.

"Okay." I still wasn't sure if it was a ploy. But Samantha had a disarming manner about her. She pulled on her cap, tucked her hair in and left the room. I stared at her as she left and then remembered the food. I was ravenous.

On the tray was a big, oval orange and a white bread roll. Next to these was a carton of apple juice, a cerise plastic cup, and some cheese wrapped in greaseproof paper. It wasn't a roast dinner, but it was perfect for me. And it all smelled great. I was so hungry.

I ate one thing after another until it was all gone. Once I'd finished, my stomach cried out for more, so I drank down the juice. It was warm but it hit the spot.

The funny thing is, it tasted like the best meal I've ever had. It was just like the packed lunches I used to take to school but ten times better. I always made my lunch from simple stuff that was easy to put together in a rush in the morning. Dad never made me any food. He was useless. I was the one in charge of cooking, when I bothered to do it. So, I liked to keep it simple.

I lay on the bed and rolled onto my back, the happiest I'd been since I got here. I let my thoughts run free. Samantha could be an ally, or she could be the good cop in a good cop, bad cop routine. And Samyaza was the bad one.

But surely, she was the enemy and was very likely to be lying to me? The enemy always lies. It was just a fact. Why would anyone want to be a Dream Fighter and work for Samyaza?

Obviously, Lake had been taken in by them. He was an idiot for getting fooled so badly. Where's his brain? I blame Kumiko though. He obviously likes her. Samantha's clearly an idiot finding herself working for them. But the evil army has a way of convincing you that you should join them. Lies and more lies. You kind of get sucked in.

But if what she said was true, that she didn't want to be doing this, then they must be blackmailing her like they blackmailed me last year. They must have something on her. Or they kidnapped a family member. Something like that. There was something genuine about her. Or else she was a really convincing actor. Maybe she would lull me into a false sense of security then get me to swear allegiance to Samyaza. Something like that. While it wasn't gonna happen.

I started having dreams of escape. My head filled up with

plots and plans. What if Samantha gave me her uniform and cap? We're about the same size and shape. She could pretend I overpowered her and left her in the cell. Would she risk her life for me? Probably not.

Maybe she could leave my door open? It would be an honest mistake. She could slip me a map of the building. If it was Daniel's house it couldn't be that complicated, right? I've had the grand tour already. And how hard would it be to get a floor plan? Okay, not that easy. Escape wasn't impossible though. I already had a sharp knife and I could use my tray to knock someone out. Yup, my English teacher Mrs Baker would be proud of me, thinking out of the box like this.

The food is making me sleepy, so I'm just going to finish writing this bit. I don't think it was drugged though. Not like the time in Zed's house when he gave me tea laced with sleeping pills and sung his creepy finger songs. This sleep feels more natural, like the blood is rushing to my stomach to deal with the food. Sleep is very welcome. It feels like a while since I've slept properly. Apart from that long plane ride on the way over of course. More later.

°°°°°*12345*°°°°°

I woke up to someone putting a bag over my head. It was frightening. I struggled as soon as I realised, trying to punch the person who was doing it. My fist hit something and it felt pretty solid.

"Hey!" yelled a man's deep voice. "Quit doing that, girl." Strong arms restrained me. I could smell sacking material and body odour. Yuck.

Another voice added, "Rachel, let him do it. We need to take you to the shower room. We don't mean you any harm." It was Samantha.

I complained bitterly. Why didn't they wake me up nicely and ask if I wanted a bag over my head? Or a shower? What's wrong with a blindfold? I'd be happy with a blindfold. What kind of danger am I to them?

Samantha said in a matter-of-fact way, "There's no point resisting. Dream Fighters follow orders. And so should you."

Samantha wasn't as nice as she made out. She had me convinced for a while though. My mistake. I shouldn't trust her. Not one bit. I don't have any friends here. I'd be a fool to think I did.

They dragged me out of the room, pulling me like a dog on a leash.

Chapter 5

They carted me off down the corridor. A bag over my head like one of those terrorist prisoners. Someone strong pulled me by the arm. It must have been the Dream Fighter man. It was cold in the corridor. Cooler than my cell.

We turned a couple of corners and I kept pace. It was quite a long walk, maybe four or five hundred steps. Maybe more. I lost count. Anyway, I played the good prisoner and stumbled along, the sack blocking my vision. It smelt of straw and muffled the sound around me. I heard the dull thud of our footsteps and a muted conversation between the Dream Fighters. I couldn't really make out the words.

They led me up some steps. They could have been made of stone or wood, I wasn't sure which. I couldn't feel any walls on either side of me. So, either they were leading me up the middle, or it was a big, wide staircase. I stumbled a couple of times. They didn't let me fall though. It's funny how you rely on all your senses when you walk. It gets harder if you don't have one or more of them.

At the top, they turned me to the right and we walked a bit further. Then we came to a stop. One of them pulled off my sack. I saw a big, mean-looking Dream Fighter on one side of me. Samantha was on the other side. The man had black, curly hair and a big barrel chest. He was unshaven and unhappy. He had a nasty, dark-blue tattoo on his neck that looked like he'd done it himself with a biro. He grunted and left us both alone. This was a relief.

"The shower's in there. It's hot, so be careful. You can take your time," said Samantha.

I decided not to be rude because I really wanted a shower. "Okay, thanks," I mumbled.

Then she said, "We've got a towel and a change of clothes in there. Oh, and there's shampoo and body wash on the floor. Like I said before, we're not animals."

"I'll take your word for it."

I took the opportunity to look around but didn't see anything much. I was in a room, much like my prison cell, with whitewashed walls. The floor was tiled. Teal and cream tiles. Not unpleasant. I couldn't hear anything much. Some distant footsteps, perhaps. The roar of a heating system, I guessed. The sounds were muffled. This could mean we're underground, but I really don't know.

Oh yeah, I have to tell you about the shower. It was amazing. I decided I absolutely love hot jets. They gushed over me, cleansing me from head to toe. My skin was alive with the sensation. The body wash smelled strongly of lavender. Little pleasures.

It was such a long time since I'd had a hot shower. I think it was back home, after I woke up from the incident with the Malkin. I closed my eyes and pointed my face upwards into the jets, trying to forget that vicious imitation of my mother. The water pressed my hair back, soaking me completely. I relaxed and tried not to think about the fact I was a prisoner.

Since that evil encounter with the Malkin, I'd hiked through the mezzanine, swum in a dangerous river and battled a blizzard. And now I was a prisoner of the enemy.

I took my time in the shower. My mind drifted away and I remembered my pool: Rachel's Pool in the mezzanine, amongst the rocks. The water that came crashing down. The presence of the Dunamis surrounding me like the water in a heated hot tub. I recalled the blazing eyes of the King. Eyes filled with love. I felt

24

a stirring within. Was he with me?

"Okay, time's up," called Samantha from outside. "Dry and dress now. Put on your new clothes. Leave your old stuff behind."

"Will I get it back?"

"No."

"Do I get another shower tomorrow?"

"I don't know. No more questions."

"I'll be out soon. Can you give me a minute?"

"I said no more questions."

"Whatever."

I turned off the water. As I started to dry myself, I felt tears slipping down my cheeks. I mopped them up, then towel-dried my hair. I didn't want her to see me crying. I had to appear strong.

My new clothes were clean and comfortable. Everything fitted just fine. Simple underwear. Midnight-blue tracksuit bottoms. A black cotton shirt and slate-grey hooded top. Nothing too unfashionable, fortunately. They also gave me a thick pair of indigo socks. These doubled as footwear.

When I came out, Samantha was still on her own. I wondered if they realised I wasn't such a big threat after all. I glanced up, expecting the Dream Fighter man to arrive any minute. Meanwhile, I tried to reason with Samantha about the blindfold.

"Do I really need that sack over my head?"

She looked at me blankly.

"I mean, I'm not going to run anywhere. Where would I go anyway? I'll keep my eyes closed if you want."

Without replying to me, she brought out a mobile phone and pressed a couple of numbers.

"Karluma? It's me. I'll handle this. You stay and relax for a bit. I'll report back in ten."

She put the phone back in her pocket and turned to look at me. Her expression was serious. "Okay, but you'd better behave. Or else."

"I promise."

As we walked, I did my best to take in every detail of our

journey, every doorway and intersection, in case it was useful later on when I made my escape. We walked down the steps. I was right. It was a broad stone staircase.

It led down to a long corridor that went in both directions. We took a left turn. Then another. The walls were smooth and white, like all the walls in this place. Yellow lights shone down at regular intervals. They were like the one in my cell. I wasn't sure if we were in Daniel's house, but you never know. He might have an underground dungeon complex. Who knows? He did once work for Samyaza after all.

"Do you have Lake?"

"A lake? What?"

"No. Lake Emerson. He's a good-looking guy about our age. Got hair the colour of treacle, you know: browny-blonde. And a cute grin."

"No questions Rachel. I said no questions."

"Have you got him?" I asked desperately.

"No. I don't think we have him," she replied quietly. "Now, no more questions please. Or we'll both get locked up." She smiled a bleak smile.

I nodded and turned away from her.

At that moment, I saw two guards further down the corridor with another prisoner. Like me, they were wearing a pair of dark blue tracksuit bottoms and a dark, hooded top. But unlike me, a hood covered the person's head. I gasped.

Perhaps it was the realisation of the full horror of what was happening to me. These guards were my jailers, not my friends. Samantha was not my friend. She was the enemy. I was being detained against my will, and I'd done nothing to deserve it. I was a prisoner on death row with seven days to live. It was as simple and straightforward as that. Every day I was alive was one day closer to my death.

I watched as they approached. The men tramped along the corridor with heavy steps. They wore the brown, red and black leather armour of the Dream Fighter army. The surface of their jackets was dull and scuff-marked. The figure in the middle was smaller and lighter. Female. She skipped along the ground lightly, with the grace of a dancer.

As we passed, the prisoner lifted her head. It was as though she saw me. But I knew the hessian sack acted as a complete blindfold. So she couldn't have.

Suddenly, her face was level with mine. Her blind gaze followed me as she passed. We were two magnets, drawn together. She said something in a language that sounded to me like Chinese. But it wasn't out loud. It was in my head or my heart. Like when the Dunamis speaks.

She was definitely a girl, like me. Her voice was light and sharp. The string of alien words swam around in my mind. Just like my thoughts sometimes did. Sometimes I get the glitch where the same phrase goes round and round for hours. A song lyric, the punch-line of a joke or a funny name. That kind of thing, you know?

So anyway, when I heard her voice, my senses heightened. It felt like the very spirit within me welled up. I was flooded by the Dunamis. Raw power coursed through my body. Power from the King. I was a grenade, about to explode.

The other prisoner stood up tall. In that instant, we connected. Did she feel the same thing? Did I know her from somewhere? But just as quickly, we snapped apart and the connection was lost. We went our separate ways.

"Keep walking," Samantha said sternly. "Head forward and keep walking."

Chapter 6

Rachel's Diary

After she dumped me back in my cell, I didn't see Samantha for the rest of the day. In fact, nobody came to see me, which gave me loads of time to write all this. After all, there's nothing else to do. They didn't feed me anything else either. Losers.

All in all, it was a very long and boring afternoon and evening. Fortunately, I have a lot of paper, so I keep myself amused, like I say. No one seems to care what I write or draw. After all, "we're not animals," apparently. So, blah, blah, blah and on with this crazy diary.

It's late night now, going by my body clock. Which isn't really much to go on, considering I've been to the mezzanine and Bhutan, whatever time zone that is. So, by what must have been late evening, I started to feel light-headed and hungry. The stale smell of my chamber was getting to me. A lack of air. The smell of wee. Whatever.

I can usually last a long time on very little food. Me and Lara are the same. You can ask her. A few bits of salad or a bag of crisps. One or two slices of pizza for breakfast. That does us for the whole day. Some of our other friends are really envious because they need chocolate all the time. But not us.

Naturally, I started thinking about Lara. Lara the Goth. Lara the Emo. Lara with her own fashion. She was my best friend all through our childhood years. We were Rachel and Lara, Raccoon and Lemur: twins; besties; inseparable.

She's in California right now, you know: the land of sunshine and dreams. Her raven-black hair is probably peroxide blonde these days. I haven't seen her in absolutely ages. So much for best friends. I'm not even sure she'd recognise me now, with my white hair.

Next, I paced around my cell for a while. It's six big steps from my bed to the door. Five and a bit the other way. Not very big really. Smaller than my bedroom back home. Next, I did circuits that took me along the wall, over to the door, back past the toilet and over to my bed. It got crushingly dull after a while.

Later on, I tried doing some sit-ups and push-ups, since I was wearing trackie bottoms – workout gear. But I wasn't really in the mood. And I was hungry. Very hungry.

It's never really occurred to me to cry out for help. I feel it would be pointless. Now I know I'm in a series of corridors and rooms, probably underground, the idea is even less appealing. I doubt the other prisoners can help me. Not the other girl I saw or anyone else locked up in here. We are trapped and helpless. I wonder how many there are of us.

So anyway, I was sitting on my bed when the door opened, making me jump. My fear was that it would be Samyaza again. My hope was it would be Samantha. Instead, it was one of the men. A leather-clothed Dream Fighter. He wasn't carrying any food with him. I shrank away, you know, instinctively.

He had a gruff voice. "Master says: are you ready to follow him?"

"You what?" I asked.

"He will give you food and freedom. Are you ready to follow him?" asked the guard.

It seemed surreal that he was asking me this. It was very clear to me that following Samyaza did not involve any real freedom. He seemed to be ignoring the fact that I'd met Zed and the Spawners. I'd met the Angel Hunters and the Malkin as well as those hideous octopus creatures. The ones that suck the life out of you. And I also know Kumiko.

In fact, I've had more than my fill of these brainwashed, brain-dead Dream Fighters. Didn't he know all this, or at least some of it? And still he was asking me to follow him.

They're killers and psychopaths, all of them. I know what they're capable of. They blackmailed me into bombing a hotel. They tried to murder me and Iona in her car. They blow up buildings for fun and mess with people's lives. And they spread lies and fear. Am I ready to follow Samyaza? What do you think? Not a chance.

I smiled and shook my head. It made him turn on his heels and leave me alone. Nobody else came after that.

°°°°°*12345*°°°°°

So, I'm writing this a couple of hours later. After the guard left, I finally lay down and closed my eyes. I felt dizzy with hunger. My stomach was painful. I'd had enough of today. I had just six days left to live. Six days. Not even a full week. I tried not to think about it.

"Rescuer, where are you?" was my plea. With my head on the pillow, I rolled my face towards the wall. In many ways, I dreaded what tomorrow had in store for me. Are they going to continue to starve me? How long can I last? What if they decide to do something nastier to me? I really don't want to dwell on that one either.

I sat there sighing a lot and tried to push the hunger from my mind. Oh yeah, I remember. I decided to pull the hood of my top over my head. It was a snug fit. Soon, my ears were warm.

And then everything changed for me. Listen up because this bit's amazing. Really amazing.

"I am Jia Li," said a disembodied voice in my head. I'm not joking. Naturally, my eyes popped open.

"Come again?" I looked around my familiar jail cell. Nothing had changed. The yellow light was still on. The door was still tightly shut. The room was empty except for my shelf, my papers, and my toilet.

"Are you there? I am Jia Li." I worked out that the voice was in my head, and it wasn't me speaking.

"Charlie?" I asked. "Dunamis, is that you? Rescuer?"

She spelt out her name. "J-i-a. L-i." Suddenly I recognised the voice. The Chinese girl. Jia Li. Her name was Jia Li. Amazing.

"Jia Li! I can hear you! But can you hear me?"

Nothing came back. I closed my eyes and tried to picture a string of words and send them into her head. I thought of the face of a Chinese-looking girl. Someone with smooth skin, round eyes and black hair. I spoke to that person in my mind's eye.

"I am Rachel Race. Do I know you?"

I lay in silence for several tense moments.

"I am Jia Li," said the voice, eventually. "Are you there?"

Frustrated, I lay back and cleared my mind. I was desperate to connect with her again. I racked my brains. Chinese girl. Captured like me. Held prisoner in a cell. But how do I communicate with her? The minutes passed and I lay there, useless.

At last, Jia Li spoke again in my head. "You are Rachel Race? I am Jia Li. Where am I? Why are they keeping me here?"

She went quiet after this. So I sat up, picked up my papers and started scribbling. Getting all of this down. Waiting for her to talk again. I'm still waiting.

Chapter 7

Rachel's Diary

I didn't have to wait too long. Jia Li's light tones sounded in my head once again. "Are you there?"

I relaxed my mind and tried to speak to her with my thoughts. I tried to keep my words short and clear as I didn't know whether or not I'd lose the link.

"I'm here. How are we talking?"

"I don't know. This is new to me."

"Do you speak English?" I asked her.

"English? No. Only Sichuanese."

"But I understand you."

"Okay."

"Okay?"

"Yes. Okay. Did we meet earlier? Was that you?"

"Yes. It was. In the corridor. I saw you. With the guards." I kept my sentences short so she got them through all right.

"I felt you. When you passed. Something happened," she said.

The connection between us seemed to be holding for the moment.

"Me too. I think it was the Dunamis. Do you know him?" I asked quickly.

"No. I don't know that name."

"Oh."

I lay still and thought for a while. "Do you know the Rescuer?"

There was a long pause. I waited. My spiteful room light beamed at me. It never goes out. I can't stand it.

"Rescuer? I know him. Rescuer is King."

"You know the Rescuer?" I asked. I felt stunned at the news.

"He rides a white horse. His face is kind. His eyes. They are like lightning."

Tears welled up and flowed out suddenly. I couldn't do anything to stop them. Two days of tension, fear and frustration. It all dissolved in tears. Funny that. Crying is such a simple and effective thing. So, I cried. A lot.

In the past, I used to cry with sadness, loneliness, desperation. I cried all the time. I guess my friends found it boring in the end. I know I was a nightmare for them. They never knew what to do with me. Anyway, these tears were different. Jia Li knew my Rescuer King: the one who made me new. Fixed me up. Made me stronger.

This changed everything. My mind filled with the possibilities. It meant everything was going to be okay in the end. It was exactly what I needed to know. Even though we were locked up, it didn't matter. They could starve me for seven days if they wanted to. I really hoped they didn't.

It was like in the mezzanine with the Angel Hunters coming at me. They could kill my body if they chose to. But the rest of me? The part that really counted? My spirit? That was out of their control. It was way out of bounds. Protected.

I was getting sleepy. But I really wanted to carry on talking to Jia Li. It felt so good to have a friend.

"I need to sleep. And I need to write this all down. But why don't you tell me about yourself, Jia Li?" I asked, frantically scribbling these notes.

"I will tell you. If you tell me about yourself as well."

"It's a deal."

"I am Jia Li. I come from Chengdu. You know it?"

"No, sorry. I don't."

"It's in China. I am sixteen years old. I had to leave my family.

It wasn't my fault. I live in the mountains with my community. High up. The bad men came to my house. They killed my friend Ri. He's dead. He tried to fight them with his sword. The Sapana took me. I surrendered to them. I hope I saved Ancoo and Lin and Chen. I don't know if the men went back."

"I am so sorry to hear that," I said. "Who are the Sapana?"

"The guards here."

"Dream Fighters. I know them as Dream Fighters."

"Okay. That's all for now."

"Really?"

"Yes. May I tell you a poem?"

Slightly surprised, I replied: "a poem? Yes, I'd like that. Mind if I write it down as well?"

She ignored me. "It is Du Fu. He is my favourite. You know him?"

"No, sorry."

"This one is very old. Sighs of Autumn. From around the year seven fifty."

"Okay."

Suddenly, the words came. My thoughts chased them as they appeared, like wind whipping up empty plastic bags on the street.

"In autumn rain, the grasses rot and die, Below the steps, the jueming's colour is fresh. Full green leaves cover the stems like feathers, and countless flowers bloom like golden coins."

She continued, "The cold wind, moaning, blows against you fiercely. I fear that soon you'll find it hard to stand. Upstairs the scholar lets down his white hair. He faces the wind, breathes the fragrance, and weeps."

The words leave an imprint on my mind. "That's beautiful," I say.

I imagine the scholar to be the Rescuer, weeping over us.

Jia Li is singing now, softly. Mainly to herself. A haunting, alien tune. I am very sleepy.

Okay, that's enough now.

Chapter 8

Rachel's Diary

Day 2. I groaned and woke up. My stomach ached. Empty. Today is my second day in this horrible little cell. The first thing I did was try and connect with my new friend, Jia Li. I closed my eyes and pictured her face, not that I know what she looks like.

"Jia Li. It's Rachel. Are you there?"

Nothing.

It was a long wait until anything interesting happened. I spent most of my time counting things. I counted my breaths, my steps, and the number of cracks in the walls. Every so often, I tried Jia Li, but I couldn't speak to her or hear from her. I couldn't feel the presence of the Dunamis either. I felt weak, alone and miserable.

Samantha came and visited me at some point. She had a red mark on her face. Just under her eye. When I saw it I raised my eyebrows.

"Don't ask," she snapped.

"It was the blindfold wasn't it? It was because you let me off wearing that sack after the shower." I felt sorry for her. And a little responsible.

"I said 'don't ask'. And I don't need your sympathy," she said coldly. "Listen up. They say I can give you some food."

"Great."

She stiffened. "But you know what you have to do to get it. Just say the four words."

"Samantha. I'm not going to do it. There's no way."

"It's just four little words."

"You know it's more than that."

"It's not so bad, you know. Living on this side of things. The war's over anyway. Samyaza's won. His Grigori and Nephilim are in every country. Every nation in the whole world. It's over. They're in charge now."

I scoffed and looked away.

"There is no point in resisting. At least this way, you get to live. Eat and shower. Stop living like an animal."

"And whose fault is that?"

"Have a semi-normal life. All he wants is for people to do the right thing and follow him. For me, I get their protection and my own room. And you could too."

I stared at Samantha. She seemed totally convinced of what she was saying.

"I have my own room," I shot back, waving my hand at the walls on either side.

"Listen Rachel. You need to be careful. They are very powerful. And he can do incredible things. Things you wouldn't believe. The world has never seen anything like it before. Nothing can stop him. If you join us, you'll get your freedom back. You can be free."

"Free? You mean like you?" I scoffed.

She stared at me for a while. "Well I've done my job anyway. Your decision is down to you."

"You got that right."

She turned to go. "There's no food today," she added, rather cruelly I thought. I wanted to jump on her and pull her hair. Run at her and thump her in the back of the head.

Instead, I folded my arms and peppered her with questions. "Tell me about the other prisoners. How many have you got? Are we underground? Under Lytescote Manor. We are, aren't we? How about the Chinese girl? Tell me about Jia Li."

She spun around to stare at me, knitting her brows. "How do

you know about her?" she asked slowly.

"Sneak me some food and I'll tell you," I answered.

"I can't do that. I'm sorry." She left.

I gave myself a quiet telling off. Samantha is your jailer not your friend, Rachel.

As she closed the door, a scream scrambled out from the back of my throat and into the light, startling even me.

°°°°°12345°°°°°

It's now later on, a lot later: possibly eleven at night. Good news. I heard from Jia Li again. It's exciting but I feel weak with hunger. I collapsed on the bed and listened to her voice in my head.

"It is Jia Li. Are you there Rachel?"

I closed my eyes. "It's so good to hear from you. I can't tell you how good."

"How are you?"

"Not good. They're starving me. I'm tired. How are you?"

"They took me out today. They want me to follow him."

"Me too. What did they do?" I asked.

"They haven't harmed me. They took me to a place where they gather. I have seen these things before in the mountains. The bad spirits fly. They do their evil magic. They have a big stone. They want me to be impressed. They want me to follow him."

"What did you say?"

"I will not follow him. I have decided to follow Rescuer. Only Rescuer."

"Same here. We are sisters."

"Sisters?" came the reply.

"Yeah, sisters. We are together in this. To the end."

We were silent for a while.

Then I asked: "Do you think they will take me to the place? The place where they fly?"

"I don't know. You don't want to go there. It is a bad place."

37

"Hold on." I felt my stomach lurch. I was so queasy. Then I was sick in the toilet. Nothing much came up. My chest heaved all the same. It was agony. My whole front ached horribly, still does. I wrapped my arms around my middle. This helped soothe it a little. But I felt rotten.

"Are you all right, Rachel Race?"

I rolled onto the bed and groaned. "No. I'm not okay. I was just sick. I feel terrible."

"I am sorry."

"Oh, that's okay. It's not your fault!"

I've still got painful cramps now. They kind of crept up on me. They sat on my chest and belly and stayed there. My body's basically at war with itself. This was how I got to spend the rest of my second miserable day of captivity. I don't have anything else to report and I need to sleep now. I'll maybe write more later, depending on how I feel. Don't hold your breath though.

°°°°°*12345*°°°°°

It was all over the web. Hastily-shot footage. Snapshots captured from a distance. The central object slightly blurred due to an extended zoom or unsteady hand. Millions of people saw them. The invaders.

One image freeze-framed an attacker. It was in São Paulo, Brazil. The dark figure hovered above the skyscrapers. Fire rained down on the street below. The tall buildings burned. The streets below: carnage.

In Alexandria, Egypt, phone video footage showed a huge monster on the rampage. Only just resembling a human. It stomped around and roared in the Bibliotheca Alexandrina. Tossed aside a human leg as people fled. Flames and chaos reigned. The masses screamed.

At the Ngorongoro Crater, Tanzania, somebody filmed a titan of a being, standing in the crater itself. The recording panned upwards. Its head reached the clouds. It was almost too pale to come out on video. The clothes of the angelic creature wafted gently, as if on the breeze. The sound was of an ethereal orchestra playing the music of the spheres.

In Volgograd, Russia, someone snapped a Warrior Angel battling a demonic winged monstrosity. This scene was mirrored in a Boston mall, the Gobi Desert and on a cruise ship sliding through the Indian Ocean. Swords clashed against talons and leathery wings. Humans shrank back, dwarfed by the intruders.

All digital lines of communication were ablaze with chatter, though web access was intermittent. People voiced their fears, swapped survivor stories and speculated wildly. The world was under attack. Aliens had come. Most people were confused. Scared. Perplexed. The end of the end was near. People were running. People were hiding. Nowhere was safe.

Samyaza sat back in Daniel's chair and grinned like a corpse. Everything was going to plan.

Chapter 9

Day 3. I reckon if I had a mirror, my face would be green. I felt sick. My lips were dry. I didn't want to get up out of bed. In fact, I wasn't even sure if I could. My eyes hurt. My head hurt. My stomach was burning inside. I thought I was going to die. Food poisoning, I thought. They fed me a poisoned apple and roll, or maybe that cheese was off.

There was a big bottle of water in the middle of my room. Just standing there. It looked clear enough. It took most of my strength to fetch it and return to the bed. It was heavy. I tore off the cap and poured some cool liquid down my throat. It revived me a little and it felt good to have something inside my stomach.

After that, I snoozed for a while. You know what it's like when you have food poisoning or the flu? Well, I felt like that. Lethargic. Aching. Unhappy. I dozed for a while, like I said.

Then I woke up out of a dream, head throbbing, and looked up. There was a Dream Fighter standing in my room. He had his arms folded, waiting patiently. Do I have no privacy? Obviously not. Samantha was standing next to him. Her expression was hard to read.

"Will you follow Samyaza?" she asked in a dull voice. That question again. I shook my head slowly.

The guard approached me with a sack in his hand. I worked out it was time to go somewhere. Shower? Execution? Maybe something else. I didn't fight them, but let them slip the hood over my head. I think I've remembered all this right, anyway.

So, they took me down the corridor to another room, much like my own. It smelt damp. A bit like mushrooms. They put me in a chair facing a huge blank screen. I lent heavily on the arms, propping myself up.

I prepared myself for torture through TV. It wasn't something I'd thought about before. Some movies can be pretty horrendous, but using videos to torture people was new to me. The US army apparently does it with death-metal, but I think I'd most likely enjoy that.

They left me alone in the room, knowing I couldn't do much damage. This was the longest I'd ever gone without food. If they wanted to kill me now, it wouldn't take much to do it.

The screen glowed. I saw a girl looking at me. She was sitting in a chair in a room like this and wearing a coffee-brown and khaki coloured Dream Fighter's uniform. I instantly recognised her as Lara. My so-called best friend. A little bit more gaunt, perhaps. A year older, definitely. Her hair was still black: scraped back into a ponytail. She still had that 'don't talk to me' expression, which I used to kind of admire. She didn't have any make up on, which was unusual for her. But then again, people change, right?

"Lara, what you up to?" I groaned. The TV must have picked it up, because she responded to me.

"Hey Rachel. Long time no see. You look the worst."

"Blame my hosts."

I focused on her face. She looked anorexic. Unhealthily so.

My heart ached for my old friend. This was the cruellest torture. Through the years we'd laughed and fought like sisters. We had shared every opinion we had on boys, food, clothes and music. At times, we'd shared a brain and freaked our friends out. We did this thing where we'd have a conversation in front of people, but do half a line each. Finish each other's sentences. Made us laugh. Drove people mad.

But I had to tell myself this figure in front of me was not my

Lara Lemur. This was an impostor. Someone I really didn't want to listen to. I knew what she was going to tell me, anyway. I didn't want to hear it. I tried to put her off as long as I could.

"So, tell me about California. What's it like?"

She smiled a thin smile. Then she said, "I like the beach like I thought I would. The ones further south, not Venice Beach. Although that's pretty amazing for different reasons. The weather has been really great. When we got here, I learned to surf down at Laguna. The waves aren't too crazy but it does get crowded."

"But then this summer, those idiotic Rescuer followers went and brought down a bunch of skyscrapers in central LA. Central LA for crying out loud. Imagine the death toll. Everything changed. Did you hear about that? I guess you did. I heard about what happened to Griffton. Shocker. If it wasn't for the Dream Fighters, we'd all be nowhere. In fact, I reckon the whole world would be in an even worse state." She rolled her eyes.

It looked like Lara. It even sounded like my cynical, Lara. But the words coming out of her mouth were not the sort of thing Lara would say.

I had to fight back. Put her right. Snap her out of it.

"Lara. It's a bunch of lies. The Dream Fighters are the ones behind it. It's all Samyaza. It's his plan. They're evil, Lara. And they're lying to you. It's not the people who follow the Rescuer at all. They're the good guys." I suddenly felt exhausted and slumped back in my seat.

Lara sneered and grinned, condescendingly. "Yeah. Sure. Thing is, Rachel, they told me you'd say all this stuff. But you're the one who's confused. They mess with your mind if you spend any time with them. It's a kind of brainwashing they do."

She went on: "But I've seen enough evidence now, and I know what's going on. It's definitely those Rescuer and Dunamis people. Listen Rach, you have to join the Dream Fighter army. We're strong. We can make a difference in the world. You and me. And you need to follow Samyaza. It really is the only way. Those other guys are close to taking over the world. And they want to destroy it. I've seen those monsters attacking the people. The black creatures with the wings and the claws. They kill people indiscriminately. No one is safe anymore."

On and on it went. "The Rescuer is the one behind it. He wants to destroy our way of life. All our values. The stuff that matters to us. Freedom of choice and the right to live life the way we want to. He's an evil dictator. He says his way is the only way. Imagine that! I've heard people say it."

She continued, "But it's a trap, Rachel. They're the reason they burned the religious books and stamped out all irrational beliefs in the past. And once again, it's risen up to destroy us. They're a cancer. An evil cancer. It's a fight to the end. A fight for our freedom."

I groaned, but it turned into a frustrated scream. "No, Lara. That isn't right. Those black creatures are Samyaza's demons. I saw them before."

"Where?" said Lara, fixing me with her gaze.

"I saw them in the other place. The mezzanine world, where they came from."

"Oh, you are crazy Rachel. And confused. But do yourself a favour. Get your head straight. Listen to these guys. Get with the programme. Make a choice to follow Samyaza. Only he can put a stop to it all."

I found myself gazing at a blank screen. Wretched and weak, all I could do was cry.

Chapter 10

Rachel's Diary

The day didn't get any better either. In fact it got worse. But not straightaway. Of course, when my jailers returned and asked the usual question, I politely declined. Weak and confused though I may be, I am still in my right mind, not like Lara. They turned her into a robot, which is alarming. But they aren't doing it to me.

Instead of starving me, the powers that be (in other words Samyaza) decided to feed me again. It was all part of his game. In my cell, on my return, was a table with some hot vegetable soup and a loaf of white bread on it. A cake and a banana sat to one side. Healthy, healthy.

There was a chair by the table. I was told to sit there and eat the food in my own time. I decided not to argue about it.

They watched me sit down then left me alone in the room. The aroma that came up from the soup almost knocked me out. My stomach was doing gymnastics. I was nervous that this was another trap. But nobody came back in, so I helped myself to it.

It was the best, tastiest dinner I've had in my life. I could taste potatoes and carrots and something that could have been sweet butternut squash. Warmth spread through my body. My head felt hot.

They seemed to know when I finished the food and came in to take away the table and chair. Then they left me alone again.

It was hard to keep the food down, but lying on my bed helped.

I didn't question why they decided I was worthy of food. After all, I hadn't done what they wanted me to. Didn't really make any sense to me.

Could this be the start of preferential treatment? Had they finished with the tough bit? Were they moving on to the next phase? Was that my final meal? It was impossible to double-guess them.

As I rested, my friend's voice appeared in my head.

"Hello Rachel. It's Jia Li."

"Hi Jia Li. Are you okay?"

"Today, they beat me."

"I am so sorry. So sorry to hear that. Are you all right?"

"I'm alive. And you? Did they mistreat you today?"

"No. I am okay Jia Li. Today they gave me food, even though I said 'no' to following him. But I will ask the Dunamis to comfort you."

"Thank you. I need to sleep now." She disappeared.

After I finished eating, I lazed around on my bed for a while. I had nothing to do and all the time in the world to do it. A thought occurred to me. Jia Li might not be the only other person out there I could connect with. I cleared my mind and tried to send my thoughts across the jail complex.

"Is there anyone out there? This is Rachel Race." It was a crazy idea. Nobody seemed to be around in my head. I tried different things, just because I had the time.

"Tell me if you're there. All you have to do is think about me, Rachel Race, I'm a seventeen-year-old girl and I'm in a cell. Put some words in my mind. It's as simple as that."

There didn't seem to be anyone around who could communicate with me. I left it for a while, trying to think of song lyrics instead. First rock, then rap and finally country. Finding this tedious, because I couldn't actually hear the music, I returned to sending out mind signals. I reached across the furthest recesses of this underground bunker, or whatever it is. I strained to touch its furthest corners.

"I'm Rachel Race. Hello." I shot that one up through the ceiling, like an arrow.

"I'm Rachel Race. Is anyone there?" That one went out in a wiggly line, over to the far side.

A new voice came back faintly. "Yes, Rachel. It is Andwele Juma. But you can call me Ndege. I am here."

I sat up. It was a young man's voice. A boy, maybe.

"Tell me about yourself," I demanded.

"I arrived today. They are keeping me in a room. Is the Dunamis helping us to talk? Where are you?"

Our conversation was cut short. My door opened. It was Samyaza. I could smell his stench. It made me gag. So, Jia Li had given me a warning. They had beaten her and I was next. I looked at his clawed hands and steeled myself for the attack. But it didn't come.

"You must know, Rachel, that I am in charge of the whole world now. I can do anything I please," his voice was gentle. But then he roared, "I can do anything." His head twitched.

I found it hard to look at this creature that belonged in the shadows, stalking the back alleys of the dark side of town. I can't even believe I'm writing this. He belongs in a nightmare. Not in real life. But it gets worse.

"I understand that you will not follow me yet," he said. "That's fine. It's early days. I will still convince you that following me is the only option you have. Or there's always an exit," his eyes went to the knife on the shelf.

I fought hard against fear.

"No matter. This is a brief visit as I have much to do. I came to give you a gift."

Samyaza moved aside slowly as two large Dream Fighters moved into the cell. They carried a long box. With the four of us and the box in the room, there was hardly any space to move.

"Until next time," said Samyaza gently. He moved through the doorway faster than was humanly possible.

One of the Dream Fighters made a grunting sound. It must

have been the signal for them to lay down the heavy box in the middle of my room. It was made of dark wood and had metal hinges on one of its long sides.

They didn't look at me, the guards. They just left.

A table, I thought. Just what I need. A long table and no chair. The voice rose up in my head again. It was the boy, Ndege. I remember our conversation so clearly. I'll never forget it. And everything that happened next.

"Rachel Race? It is Ndege. Can you hear me?"

"I can hear you, Ndege."

"It is cold. How are you, sister?"

"They brought me a box."

"They also bought me a box."

"Really?"

"It is in my room," he said.

"What do you think it is?"

"I fear that it is some snakes."

"Snakes? Really?"

"I do not know. I just hate snakes. Should we open the boxes? Is that what they want us to do?"

"I don't really want to," I admitted.

"We shall open them together," his voice said.

"All right. But be careful. I'll count to three and then open yours. I'll open mine at the same time."

"Okay."

I stood and put my hands on the lid. I started to count in my head, sending the numbers towards my new friend.

"One. Two," I gripped the sides, preparing myself for what was inside. Not that I ever could.

"Three."

My heart stopped beating. It was too much to bear. Inside the box they had laid my dad, Eddie. Those murderers. His hair was still white and ruffled like when I saw him last. He looked asleep. But I knew he was dead. The box was a coffin. I love you dad.

The voice in my head was whimpering. "It is my father. They killed my father. He's in the box. These animals. They put him in a box."

"Yes," I said. And then I passed out.

Chapter 11

On Mount Jomolhari in Bhutan, Lake Emerson stood and marvelled at the Protector of the Air. The enormous angel stretched hundreds of feet into the clouds and shimmered like a river.

Lake was still glowing from the honour of being the one chosen to activate it. Nothing he'd ever achieved in his life came close. Not the swimming tournaments or the prize-winning front-page stories at the Griffton News; nothing compared. This was by far the greatest buzz, the best thing ever. He relaxed into the moment, wondering what its significance was for the world and for the human race.

The Protector emitted an eerie sound that wafted through the thin mountain air. Long strands of sustained notes. Some barely perceptible. It sang to the world of its presence. Lake found it hard to drag his eyes away. He felt like he was watching the slow, billowing mushroom cloud of a nuclear explosion.

"Are you really real?" He breathed. It struck him that there were two more Protectors like this one. Incredible. He wondered whether the other two groups had been successful in their missions and if they were seeing this too.

The last time he'd seen the others was in the mezzanine, near the caves. At that point, they'd divided up to tread their separate paths. Daniel, Arabella and the boys went to somewhere in the Pacific Ocean to activate the Protector of the Sea. Meanwhile, Caleb, Serena and Micah journeyed to Tanzania to find the Land

Protector. It was good the others could go somewhere warm, thought Lake. Bhutan, on the other hand, was literally freezing. It would be like pulling the short straw, if it wasn't so stunningly beautiful.

But how would he know if they'd all made it to their destinations? He dearly hoped he'd see them again. They were his new friends. His only true friends. And of course there was Rachel. Lake was desperate to hold her in his arms once more. Hug her close. It pained him that she'd been taken. And there was nothing he could do to prevent it. Losing Eddie was another major blow that weighed heavily on him. He hated the enemy and held Samyaza responsible for Eddie's death along with Rachel's kidnapping.

Freezing mountain air filled his lungs, making his chest ache. The cold, clean smell of snow and ice hung in his nostrils. Bhutan's mountain view was almost too extravagant to take in. The great rocks before him were like sleeping giants, shrouded in white cloth with long grey seams. One of them had a curved top. It dropped down at an angle to meet a series of lower peaks. They continued along the horizon: a series of undulating mounds. Frothy grey clouds rested near their summits. Cappuccino foam. These offered some respite to the eyes from the bright patches of white mountainside all around them. Just spectacular.

All the while, playing in his head on repeat was his meeting with the Rescuer. His sharp journalist's mind kept asking: "Did it really happen? What evidence do you have that the encounter actually took place? How do you know it's not all in your head?"

But he knew his heart was settled and his stomach was full. He was convinced at the core of his being that he'd met the King of the universe and eaten with him. And even further, he was sure, with an iron-clad certainty, that he was a new man. He was Lake Emerson 'mark two', a more complete, stronger, better version of himself. The Rescuer had called him into friendship with himself and filled a void inside his heart; an emptiness inside his soul.

Besides, he was staring at a real-life angel right now. What more could a news reporter ask for? If he chose to write it, it would be the story to end all stories. If anyone had faith to believe his account.

He was beginning to feel the cold. "So, what next?" He asked the Dunamis, looking around.

"Time to move on," came the reply. Lake loved hearing the voiceless voice. It was clear and quiet. Like the breeze.

"Which way?"

But Lake already knew which direction he was being prompted to move in. The path wove around the mountain he was on. He followed it, walking at a pace. After a while, his view of the valley was obscured by a wall of rock. He kept going. He was heading in roughly the opposite direction from the house where he'd rested. The place where Eddie lay. Tucked up in a thick duvet of snow.

As he descended, the ground became less icy. Charcoal-coloured rocks protruded on either side. He started to see hardy, vibrant plant life and trees. Some of the growths seemed to sprout out of the very rocks. Who knows how far down their roots travelled to find nourishment, he thought. He stopped to rest, sitting on a fat, round boulder. Beside him grew two long poppies. Their petals were iceberg-blue in colour surrounding a tangerine centre.

After a very long time, he came to a muddy path. It was the first time he'd seen signs of human habitation. Tire marks. A basic stone wall. A pile of logs. The smell of burning.

He came to a compact little village. It comprised a scattering of mud-grey houses, simple in design, with wood-framed windows. A couple of the buildings were painted cream. Lake couldn't see any people in the streets though. He was on his guard, not wanting to bump into the enemy.

"Dunamis, I'm trusting you. You're going to keep me alive, aren't you?"

The muddy track became a more pronounced path. This, in turn, became a strong, pebbly road. Lake kicked a stone and kept walking. He was getting hot in his jacket and boots but was aware his face was still frosty. If he started stripping off, he could freeze very quickly: turn into an ice sculpture there and then. Then what good would he be to anyone?

An eerie stillness covered the village. Wandering past the houses, he saw they were deserted. Some of the front doors were open. A copper-coloured brazier sat lifeless. A child's bicycle rested on its side. It was like the people had been snatched up in an alien invasion. Lake looked around him, casting his gaze backwards.

Some distance away, he saw a man standing by the side of a house, talking to another man. He wasn't alone. They were the only two people in view. Leather armour. A diagonal sash: crimson. A long scabbard: thigh level. Dream Fighters.

He knew them well from Lytescote Manor. He'd lived among them. Inhaled their stench. Suddenly, it occurred to him that these could be the men who murdered Eddie. Fear flashed through his brain.

They spotted him. Lake moved faster, turning his walk into a trot. They followed. He broke into a jog. They gave chase. He ran for his life.

Soon, Lake was pelting down the road to get away from the fierce warriors. They weren't particularly fast, weighed down by their gear, but they were persistent. "I could really do with my rollerblades," thought Lake.

"Do not be afraid," said the Dunamis.

"Really?" Lake panted, sprinting now. "I'm not meant to be afraid? Tell me how."

He looked back hastily. The men were gaining on him. Checking in front of him again, he was arrested by a towering figure planted in the middle of the road. It was black, tall and stout and grew horizontally larger as he watched it. He immediately realised he was looking at a demon creature from the mezzanine world.

Its wings stretched out to the left and right, spanning the breadth of the whole road. They were dark and powerful: a thick wall of leather. Lake was trapped between the Dream Fighters behind and an Angel Hunter in front.

There was nowhere to run.

Chapter 12

Pausing for a moment, he checked his options. Then he took a quick breath and skittered sideways, leaping off the path. Pumping his arms, he sprinted between two houses. Both had dark wooden front doors. Brown beams crisscrossed their frames.

His feet pounded a path through the powdery mud and pebbles. Chalky dust sprayed up as each foot landed.

"Look for a green door."

"What? I can't see a green door. There isn't a green door," panted Lake. Had he heard correctly?

He came out at the back of the houses where he saw a couple of huge slabs of rock and little else. The stony ground ended in the distance with a steep vertical wall of rock.

"There's no green door," he said desperately, looking in all directions. His pursuers hadn't caught up with him yet but there was nowhere to go. Not unless he broke into a house. Was it an option? If he did that, surely he'd be trapped? But what if the green door was an internal one?

Alone under the naked white sky, Lake panicked. He tried to think clearly, taking in everything he could see. Two houses. A squat wooden outhouse. Two robust boulders made of stone. Feeling the urge to hide behind them, he raced over. Ducking behind one of them, he figured he'd bought himself a couple of minutes.

He squatted down, breathing heavily, listening hard. Quiet

at first. Then footsteps in the distance. Had they seen him take cover?

The rock was big and flat, like it had sheared off from a cliff face. It did a good job of hiding him from sight. On the back someone had painted the rough outline of a house in copper-coloured paint. A childish creation. At the centre was a green door, irregular in shape.

"A green door," whispered Lake.

"Go through," the Dunamis commanded.

"Right you are. I've got nothing to lose." He grinned and pressed himself into the rock, trusting completely in that moment. "This is crazy, but it must be like the stone heads," Lake reasoned to himself.

Then he melted into the green door. He left Bhutan far behind, vanishing into thin air as far as the world was concerned.

Several minutes after he departed, one of the Dream Fighters stomped over to the rocks and peered behind them to the left and to the right. Failing to notice the painted house at the rear, he glanced up at the vertical rock face. The visitor was nowhere to be seen.

Shaking his head, he rejoined the other man who stood between the houses. They made a quick decision and split up, each choosing a building to enter and search.

Meanwhile, the Angel Hunter spread his wings and climbed the heights to look over the whole village in search of the running man. Like a drone, he drifted up level with the roofs and then rose higher, looking in every direction. But Lake was long gone.

°°°°°*12345*°°°°°

Bony pterodactyls circled high above, their angular bodies gliding through the purple clouds. On the far side of the sky, the ruby sun sat and watched the darkness which encroached like a spreading ink stain.

Lake felt like a disembodied ghost. On entering the mezzanine he instantly lost all feeling in his arms and legs. Floating along the rock-strewn path, he worried that he might fall on his face at any moment. He hoped his senses would return faster than the first time. He remembered how badly this wild place had baffled both his body and his mind.

"Where do I go?" he asked, feeling emotionally raw. Wrung out.

He faced open ground on all sides. Unlike before, when he had emerged from the stone head, there was no such landmark. This time, he'd tumbled through thin air and passed into the mezzanine like a breath.

"It's changed, hasn't it? The stone heads. That's why the one on the mountain didn't work. We don't need them anymore. So how does it work now?" He was talking out loud, his voice sounding higher pitched than usual.

Lake didn't hear any answer from the Dunamis but his thoughts ran on. And so did his mouth. "So what: can people get in and out of the mezzanine from anywhere? Does that mean that if I can slip through, so can they?"

He glanced about nervously, fully expecting an instant invasion of demons.

"No, not anywhere," came the voice of the Dunamis.

"Oh, okay. Not anywhere then. But there are places, right?"

"This way," urged the voice, which formed an impression in his mind. Suddenly, Lake found himself wrestling internally as doubt arose. His rational mind tried to work out whether the voice was real or if he was in fact generating it subconsciously. Was the mezzanine even real, or was it a figment of his imagination? He felt sick at the thought that he could be completely delusional.

"This way," said the voice in his head with the urgency of a knock at the door.

No time for questions. "I'm coming, I'm coming," he jabbered.

He bounced across the ground. It was a haphazardly-patterned plane of rocks and cracks, like so much of the mezzanine. A desert of rock and scrub, devoid of trees or hills. It ran for miles in every direction.

As Lake jogged over the stones and gaps, strength and feeling returned to his legs. Much faster than the first time. Almost at once he was overwhelmed by his senses. The air smelt of sand and mud. Loud shrieks rained down from the pterodactyls wheeling through the sky. The solid ground returned the impact of his steps. Shockwaves went up through his knees. He filled his lungs with mezzanine air. Dusty and dry. He was alive again. "Okay, this is real," he conceded.

"So, I just keep running in a straight line?"

He checked over his shoulder for signs of danger. No monsters, fortunately. But something strange was happening to the landscape. On the horizon, a cloud of dust was rising up in a horizontal line. It became a thick blanket of grey fog in the far distance closing in on him casually but persistently.

He realised in horror that the ground was falling away as the dust rose up. And it was happening in slow motion. A wide sinkhole was opening up. Sucking down the surface. Accompanying it was a continual crackling that grew into a crashing din. Lake started to run faster.

"The ground. It's disappearing." He gasped. He knew he was stating the obvious. But somehow, it was good to verbalise it. "Need your help! Quick!"

The plummeting landscape chased his heels. Roaring as it fell away. A rising crescendo. The dust like a tidal wave above his head. Ready to crash down.

"Help!" cried Lake more urgently.

He worked his arms up and down, sprinting at full pelt. He took a chance and glanced backwards. The rocks behind were sinking down into the abyss just a hundred feet away. The wave of destruction was coming for him like a tsunami. In a couple of minutes, he would be swept down into the depths. The dark bowels of this mezzanine hell.

As Lake turned to look to the front again, he took a tumble, tripping over his feet. Falling forwards, his head plunged towards the ground. He'd gone over a lot of times in the past while skating. A painful number of times. But this time he knew it would be his final fall.

Down he went. But rather than a painful collision with the ground, which had now disintegrated, it was a slow descent into darkness. He felt like he was falling from a great height, only the fall went upwards. It made no sense. And he could see nothing that gave him his bearings. It was a moment of gut-wrenching panic. Black fear.

Eventually, the darkness thinned out. He was flying above a rising dust cloud. Carried upwards by a huge white bird. Except it wasn't a bird. It was a Warrior Angel.

Chapter 13

I cried for a very long time. In fact, I spent the rest of the day crying. My third day in jail. Imagine. I looked at him for ages, lying there so peacefully. And I cried. Even though I knew he was in a better place.

Then I closed up the box, sat on the bed and cried some more. I cried until my tears ran out. Felt like it anyway. Until my mind went numb. The human mind is so amazing you know. It protects you from overloading. It lets your emotions come in waves. And I'm able to write this diary. Somehow.

I could hear his voice. He was calling me "Chicky" like he does. And he was pulling a funny face. It made me laugh to think about it. I forgot about being sad. It was like he was here with me. Alive. A while back, the shock of having him here in my cell wore off, believe it or not. Strangely, it was actually nice to have him with me. Even though I knew he was gone. I talked to him a bit. After all, why not?

I'd say, "Dad, I don't know what these people want of me. Well, I do know what they want. But they're not going to get it this way. Their approach is all wrong. They don't understand me at all. Not like you."

And he'd listen to me. At least I pretended he did. And somewhere, somehow, I knew he heard me.

Curled up on my bed, I lay watching the box. My chest hurt

58

from crying. I felt a strange weightlessness: both my parents have left the planet. I was free-floating through space. Alone without any brothers or sisters. Both my parents are gone. Lara's joined the rebel army. Lake's on the other side of the world. He's far away. So are my new friends: Micah, the Harcourt family, Caleb and Serena. I don't think I'll ever see them again. Iona is somewhere in Griffton, hopefully safe. I missed her coolness.

So anyway, somehow, in this horrible dungeon with my father in a box and the light that never goes out, I closed my eyes and felt at peace. Strange, I know.

Okay. My account of the day is almost over. But there's just one more thing I need to tell you. It's amazing. I'm sure you will agree. Here it is.

So, I looked up and saw a figure that was almost invisible but not quite. It looked like it was made of lace or gossamer. Like a wedding dress. My own Warrior Angel was standing guard over me. His head reached the ceiling and his eyes were soft. I felt the presence of the King, washing over me in waves.

I knew, in that instant, that there is evil in this world and terrible things do happen. But, at the same time, my Rescuer is good. And he loves me.

So, I'm lying here now, knowing I'm not alone. And he's soothing my broken heart. And that's how today ends. Good night.

°°°°°*12345*°°°°°

Rachel's Diary

Day 4. When I woke up, the box was gone. So was the angel.

My head was filled with chattering. A bunch of voices held a conference call in my mind. The new guy, Ndege, was telling Jia Li about his father in sad tones. Someone else new, a boy called Paolo, was also there. I learned that he recently discovered the Rescuer and made his decision to follow him and not Samyaza. He was buzzing with excitement about it all. I wondered whether the fifth person was around as well.

"Okay everyone," I said, "this is Rachel. Tell me who's here."

"Jia Li. I am here."

"It is Ndege," said my new friend.

"I am Paolo from Katowice, Poland," said the one I didn't know.

"Hey, Paolo from Katowice, Poland. Tell me about yourself," I ordered.

"They grabbed me. Like you all. They brought me to this place. I travelled by plane I think. Helicopter maybe. I don't know. I miss my mum."

"Yeah, me too," said Rachel. "Are you all missing a finger?"

"I was," said Ndege, "But he gave me a new one. The Rescuer, through his Dunamis."

I felt a pang of jealousy at this and demanded: "How did that happen?"

"A woman asked him for me. She was a prophetess. Serena. I will never forget her."

"Hold on. You know Serena? When did you see her? How is she?"

"She came to visit my country, Tanzania."

"Was she with two men, Micah and Caleb?"

"Yes, she was."

"Are they okay?"

"Yes they are. And yes, they were successful."

"You mean...?"

"Yes. They activated the Land Protector."

"Really?"

"Actually, I got to do it with Micah. It was beautiful, Rachel. We danced by the lake in the crater. An angel as big as a mountain came up from the ground. And we met a talking lion."

"It sounds incredible," Paolo chipped in.

"Do you know what happened to them?" I asked.

"No. I left them to go home. That's when they took my father."

"I am so sorry."

"It is not your fault," said Ndege.

"Does anybody know who the fifth person is?"

"What do you mean?" This came from Jia Li.

"There are five of us. Each of us lost a finger."

"I lost a thumb. Part of my thumb. It still hurts," said Jia Li. "Why did they do this to us?"

I explained, "It was a creature called Zed. A shape shifter. He used a bat monkey-bird to take them. And he created a monster called the Malkin. It had my mother's face. It was terrifying. And he sewed our fingers onto her hand."

The voices all buzzed at once. "What? Why? Really?"

"As far as I understand, it meant she could open the door in the mountains to let Samyaza out. It was in Nepal. Samyaza was being held under the Himalayas. Underground. Or something."

"I know those mountains," offered Jia Li.

"How do we stop him?" asked Ndege.

"I don't know," I admitted. "Anyone have any ideas?"

Silence fell across my mind.

"So why us? I never signed up to anything." This came from Paolo.

"You didn't. We were chosen. It's how the Rescuer works. He chooses you. Then it's up to you whether you follow him or not. All I know is the five of us are linked by our bloodline. We share a common ancestry, apparently. It's what my friend Daniel worked out. And if anyone knows, it's him. He used to follow Samyaza you know."

"So we really are sisters," said Jia Li.

"Yeah, we're sisters."

I got up off my bed and started pacing around the cell. "Connected. We're connected. By blood and spirit."

I had a think, then said, "Okay, I've got an idea. Are you ready to try something?"

They all agreed. "I've no idea if this will work. But it's worth a go. So anyway, here it is. I really hate the light in my room."

"Me too," said Jia Li.

"It's always on and it never goes out. It's so bright and I've really come to hate it. If I want to get a break from it I have to stick my head under the pillow. So here's what I want you to do. Everyone, do this at the same time. Call on the power of the Dunamis and focus on your light. Everyone doing that?"

Three voices came back, telling me yes.

"Now tell it to go out."

I heard a shattering sound from high up on the wall. A shard of glass cut my face, but I grinned anyway. I was sitting in complete, glorious darkness.

A party erupted in my mind. I breathed out and smiled. Small victories.

Chapter 14

Ben was the owner of what used to be the Rock and Shock music store before the people of Griffton smashed it up after the bombings. First of all, someone threw a rock through the window and some of his merchandise got stolen. He tidied up as best he could. Hoping he could reopen. Then the shop got hit again, even worse. Everything was beyond repair. He had to abandon it. It felt like someone had ripped his heart out.

Rock and Shock was his baby. Five years ago, he'd borrowed money from his father and built the business from scratch. Closing the shop meant losing his livelihood: everything. He knew he wasn't the only one in this situation. There was no point feeling sorry for himself. Some people had lost their lives in the past few weeks. But boy, did it hurt. It felt like his child had died. Or his closest friend. It was terrible.

Ben brandished a metal baseball bat and looked nervously around him. He was a tall man with shoulder-length black hair under a crimson baseball cap.

Stepping carefully across a long stretch of bottle-green broken glass, he thought about the high likelihood of being confronted by someone unfriendly. It was incredibly dangerous to be out alone. He was well aware of this. He heard of friends getting beaten for no reason. He also heard that people sometimes disappeared, never to be seen again. But he really wanted to check on Iona. See that she was safe.

The streets of Griffton had become a war zone. Armed groups of citizens roamed around on missions to steal supplies or carry out a beating of a suspected Rescuer follower. And that's what he was now. Ever since Iona showed him what happened to her leg and introduced him to the King. He believed Iona because he knew her and trusted her. And he loved her. So, when he encountered the Rescuer King, he was all in. But in doing so, he became a secret follower: an enemy of the state. A rebel.

It was now officially against the law for anyone to gather as a group in public. But it didn't stop some people. Especially the unsavoury kind. He longed for the days when the Zodiacs were the most evil thing around. Those boys were nothing compared to the armed and brutal thugs of today.

The gangs that were unofficially sanctioned were allied to Samyaza and the Dream Fighters. And they acted as a second army. Equally dangerous to people like Ben were the independents: heavily-armed psychopaths who did their own thing.

From time to time, these two groups, the gangs and the independents, clashed violently. As a result, there was always bloodshed. You never knew where it was going to erupt. And if the Dream Fighters were involved, they acted without mercy in clamping down on insurgency.

So, most people stayed indoors. Apart from the times when they lined up to get their rations from the Dream Fighters. Food, water, toilet rolls. Nobody dared go out to work. It wasn't much of a life.

Then, a few days ago, things got even worse. Everything went up a level when the demons arrived in the city. The invasion happened without any warning. Admittedly, Ben hadn't seen them yet. But he'd heard about them. People said they came out of thin air. Started killing people in their houses. Or in the supermarkets where people were waiting for their food. It even took the Dream Fighters by surprise, apparently. The demons were savage and ruthless. And they could fly. Nowhere was safe.

After a while, the killing stopped and most of the demons

vanished. People spotted them from time to time and tried to capture them on their phones and upload the pictures. There were also rumours of angels, but he hadn't seen any himself. There were pictures from the web though, from around the world. The angels were the only thing that could stop the demons, some people reckoned.

Like everyone else, he'd stayed in hiding at his friends' house: Sven and Agneta. He moved there when Rock and Shock was gutted and no longer safe to live in. They let him have a room out back. It had a couch and a duvet but not much else.

Earlier this morning, Iona invited him over to her house. She had a couple of other people sharing it: a married couple and a female friend. People she trusted. Rescuer followers. She was happy for them to stay. Safety in numbers. He'd met them before and they were nice people. It was important for the good guys to stick together these days, he reasoned.

Ben emerged from the Tendrils and onto the beach road, Griffton Boulevard. He had a good look around. There was one man walking away down the road. Hunched shoulders and a purposeful stride. Long ochre hair. A green army jacket. No particular threat. Apart from that, there was no one else. He lowered the bat.

Both Rock and Shock and Iona's house were on this road but he couldn't bear to see his old store in ruins again. It was just too much, so he glued eyes to the pavement as he walked past. Then he glanced out to sea. It was calm and grey this morning. White seagulls flecked the waves. The beach revealed patches of mustard sand amidst an expanse of knuckle-sized pebbles. There was more litter on the beach than he'd ever seen before.

Ben quickened his pace and arrived at Iona's door around ten thirty. He smiled broadly when he saw her. She always made him smile. In turn, she greeted him enthusiastically, kissing him on the cheek and smothering him with her wild profusion of spiral curls.

"Oh Ben, you made it," she said breathily.

"I guess walking for half an hour through Griffton without being attacked counts as an achievement these days," he said wryly.

"Come in, come in. Are you okay?"

"Yes, I'm fine. You look lovely, as usual," he said, gazing at her. Iona turned away and grinned. "The others are through here," she said. "We leave our weapons at the door," she added. Ben nodded and rested his baseball bat against the wall, next to a plank of wood.

Sitting on colourful beanbags and soft chairs were her friends, Matt, Grace and Sophia.

"We have to do something," Matt was saying, animatedly. He glanced nervously at Ben as he entered, and then said, "Ah, Ben, hi! I was just saying we can't just sit around doing nothing. You agree with me, don't you?"

"It's not that I disagree," said his wife, Grace. "It's just that it's so dangerous. We're not fighters. I mean, you're a tax adviser, sweetie."

"I was a tax consultant. But not anymore. We're all soldiers now. We don't have a choice. Everything changed for me when they took me and put this thing in my neck."

"Did you ever work out what it was?" asked Iona with her eyes wide.

Matt replied, "Not really. Some sort of chip they said. For my own good. If they wanted to kill me, I guess they would have. And if it's a tracker, they'd probably be here with their guns."

Iona looked alarmed.

"But instead they let me go free." He rubbed the back of his neck with his right palm. "One thing stayed with me though. They did say they've changed my name. I thought that was really odd. And presumptuous. What am I, a baby?"

"What's your name now," Iona asked.

"Kom, apparently." He shrugged. "Bit like 'Tom'. To be honest, it's a total mystery and not something I want to think too much about." He looked tired. "I'd rather talk about how we can stop them."

"Okay. So, what's the plan?" asked Ben. "I've got my baseball bat."

Matt slumped back. "No plan yet. I'm not suggesting we attack the army barracks. But we have to do something. How about we make contact with the angels? They seem to know how to deal with Samyaza's monsters from what I'm seeing on the web. Maybe they can help us."

"We definitely need some help. What do you think Iona?"

Iona made her eyes huge. "I really don't know. And I can't believe I'm saying this, but I really wish Rachel was here. She'd know exactly what to do."

Chapter 15

This was way up there on his list of mind-blowing things, thought Lake. In fact, he would put it a close second to meeting the Rescuer, or activating the Protector in the mountains. It was almost as much a thrill as diving under those rocks in the mezzanine and coming out the other side alive.

The angel, Jerahmeel, carried him higher into the mezzanine sky, the cool air making him shiver. The feeling of flight was so much more intense than skating or surfing. His head rushed and his body buzzed. His face was numb, his lips dry.

Meanwhile, he tried to take everything in through his eyes: pterodactyls, purple clouds and the ground far below. There was so much to see.

A pale band of river shimmered, meandering through the blood-red valley. The ground was darkened by cloud shadow in some places. Speckled in others with hundreds of grey shadow-patches cast by rocks that hung in the air.

Lake and the angel flew over a gleaming city built from translucent glass; like an ice-cube metropolis. Lake was instantly awed: filled with wonder beyond words. A thick circular wall surrounded the city. Each building was fashioned like a cathedral: ornate and multilayered. He tried to take in the details but it was just overwhelming.

The wall itself was made of a pink substance resembling coral. It had glass needles that rose high into the air. Incredible, thought

Lake. He learned that it was an angel city. But they weren't due to stop there. He was left aching to see more of this other-worldly place.

They travelled on. Lake enjoyed the rhythmic beating of the angel's wings. The sound was reminiscent of a skipping rope moving in slow motion. He guessed it was the closest to being a bird that he'd ever get. So he relaxed and tried to keep the fear from his mind. The fear of falling thousands of feet to his death. And as he let go, he felt overwhelmed by the peace and joy of the Dunamis.

Ice-capped mountains appeared. They were made of dark red rock. At their feet grew a broad forest of fire-red trees. The angel brought them lower. Lake noticed some of them grew sideways, forming a criss-cross of tangled branches.

They approached an oval basin-shaped valley, long and shallow, sloping up towards a collection of rocky hills. At the other end, in the far distance, a red desert reached into infinity. He saw a solitary stone head marking the end of the basin and the start of the desert.

Jerahmeel set him down gently on the ground which was dusty underfoot. Lake thought he recognised the place. He was sure he'd been through that ten-foot stone head. Yes: he remembered being at Griffton Cliff one minute and inside the mezzanine the next.

As Lake stood and recovered from his flight, he had a good look at the angel. He observed that under his garment he was muscular like a bodybuilder. His face was on the edge of indescribable: full of beauty and peace. Innocent. His clothes were alive, flashing with light. At his waist was a long sword, resting in a jewelled scabbard.

"Man, that was amazing. Can we do it again?" He removed his backpack and coat and plopped them down. Suddenly tired, he joined them on the ground, stretching out his legs in front of him. It felt good to stop but he sensed it wouldn't be for long.

"This region of the mezzanine is safe at the moment. We can

talk," said Jerahmeel. His voice was like a set of wind-chimes, or streams of water running through a forest.

"I've been here before, haven't I? Is Zed's house up there at the end of the valley?"

"Yes, he chose this place to dwell. But he is gone now."

"Dead?"

"Yes and his sons are no more. You are safe from them."

"Yes, of course. I saw you guys finish them off. Good thing too. So, is this how I get back home? Is my doorway nearby?"

"When we have completed our conversation, I will show you the way. Things have changed. The former doorways no longer work."

"Ah, I knew it. So tell me," Lake spoke more quietly. "How is Rachel? Is she okay?"

"Rachel Race is being held by Samyaza. As for her well-being, I do not know."

"So you don't know if they've harmed her?"

"The Rescuer loves her and he is with her."

"Okay. Do you know where she is?"

"No."

"How about the others? Did they activate their Protectors? Did they see what I saw?"

"Yes."

"So what do they do?"

"The others or the Protectors?"

"The big angels – the Protectors."

"Like us, the Protectors are servants of the most high. When they are required, they will act."

"So, what will they do?"

"That is not mine to say."

"Do you know about my friends? Where are they?"

"They have not departed from their locations."

"Are they safe?"

"No human is safe. Our enemies roam the earth. Angel Hunters walk freely in your world. Samyaza and his Nephilim are oppressing the nations. This world can no longer offer safety. But take heart, because victory is assured. Samyaza is already defeated. And so he was from the beginning of time."

"I don't understand."

"These things are mysteries, Lake Emerson."

"Hmm."

"Our time has come to an end now. You must leave."

"Really? So soon? But I still have questions. A lot of questions. Is Kumi still working with Samyaza? How do we stop him?"

"You need to walk towards that tree over there now. The Dunamis is with you."

Lake turned to look. It was one of the fire-red trees growing diagonally out of the ground. Like someone had driven into it with a truck and knocked it over. He didn't know how he managed to miss it before. Up close, he noticed back stripes running along the trunk. Zebra stripes.

"So, I just walk towards it?" But the angel was on his way up, beating his broad wings like an eagle. Lake watched him becoming a dot, travelling in an arc under the magenta clouds. He turned back to check the tree was still where he'd left it. Fortunately, it was.

"Okay tree, it's you and me then. Tree-mendous. Let's go."

With his backpack on one shoulder and his coat bundled over his left forearm, he stepped gingerly towards the tree. Three steps later he passed out of the mezzanine.

He found himself dwarfed by tall buildings. They were instantly recognisable. Griffton City Bank. The blue-tinted office building shared by the software giants. He was home again.

Chapter 16

The smell of seaside city air washed over him. A seagull squawked. A warm day. Afternoon, or possibly early evening. Summertime.

There was a faint melody as ambient music played several streets away. The dull, repetitive thud of a synthesized drumbeat. Lake didn't recognise the tune. Apart from that, it was relatively quiet. Griffton city centre was usually so busy. Especially on a nice summer afternoon like this. But there were no big groups of people laughing and chatting at the tables outside the wine bars as there should be. No packs of tourists shuffled along today, taking selfies. No sounds of traffic. Dead like four in the morning.

He spotted a handful of individuals and maybe four or five couples walking with purpose. They kept their heads down. And to his right and left, he noticed the heavy presence of Dream Fighters. He froze in alarm.

But they weren't after him, unlike the ones in Bhutan. And, fortunately for him, they didn't have a telepathic connection or a hive mind. Otherwise they'd have pounced on him already. Instead, they stood in units of two, glaring at the people, keeping order by glowering and clutching their weapons. He was fine for the time being.

As he stood in the doorway they looked right through him. This must be what it feels like to be a ghost, thought Lake. Regardless, he made sure he didn't catch their eyes, just in case.

He watched them for a while as they gazed around slowly,

looking for signs of trouble.

"Okay, Dunamis," he muttered under his breath. "I'm back home. Where do I go?"

"Wherever you choose."

"Right you are then. The Griffton News is round the corner."

Keeping his eyes down on the pavement, he started walking north. It took him towards one of the pairs of guards, but they didn't seem to be stopping anyone. He decided he'd take his chances.

"Halt citizen," barked one of the Dream Fighters just as Lake passed him. He tensed. One had a sword and the other a gun. He turned to the man who had spoken. He was tall and unshaven with a scar on his cheek. Lake felt he recognised him, perhaps from Lytescote Manor. He lived there for a week, so there was a strong possibility he would be captured and tortured by Kumiko if this went the wrong way. He kept his eyes averted.

The soldier stared at him for a long time. Lake tried to keep cool. "Give me your bag," he finally ordered.

Lake handed it over without an argument.

The Dream Fighter took his time rummaging through it. Lake whistled quietly. He knew he didn't have much in there. Clothes and toiletries. Certainly not a gun or a knife. He counted the seconds while the man went through everything.

After a while, he demanded: "Where have you come from?"

"Friends." Lake looked down at the ground.

"Where are you going?"

"Home," he responded without skipping a beat. He took a chance and had a quick glance at the man's eyes. They were tired and bored.

"All right. Move on," he ordered. "Stay indoors. It's safer."

Lake took his bag slowly and gently. He nodded to the soldier. Then he continued on his way. Once he was clear of them, he let out a breath which blew softly through his lips like a raspberry.

"Dunamis, that was too close for comfort," he mumbled.

Ten minutes later he was staring at the gutted shell of the

73

Griffton News tower. He gawped at it, overwhelmed by emotions. Rooted to the pavement. Like the police station bombing he'd covered for the newspaper, this too was a mangled mess of masonry, metal and glass.

The top of Mike Wright's whiteboard was sticking out of a pile of grey rubble. Lake could just about read the list of top-five stories, written in red capital letters in Mike's writing. The first of them was: "Dream Fighter brutality on Griffton streets." He saw bodies in the debris and felt conflicted about whether he should rush in and unearth them. But nothing was moving.

Lake turned away. In one single blow, Samyaza had hit at everything he held dear. His friends and colleagues. The job he loved. Free speech and a free press. Journalistic stories and daily news. Who he was as a person. A man of truth.

He was also faced by the fact he'd betrayed his friends to work for the enemy. And then he'd betrayed Kumiko. One betrayal followed by another. So, she wreaked her revenge on him. But it was his fault. Because of Lake she'd destroyed the Griffton News and killed his friends at the same time. Maybe even Mike who'd escaped Samyaza's prison camps. He may never get the chance to tell everyone he was sorry. He closed his eyes, a sob rising up his throat. Guilt, responsibility, sorrow, hopelessness. They fell over him like an avalanche.

"It's not fair," he whispered. The destruction of his building was completely disproportionate. An act of ugly vengeance. Petty and nasty. Just like Kumi. Just like Samyaza. Nothing about it was okay. He suddenly felt unbearably tired.

Lake trudged like a dead man walking from the city centre to his parents' house on the east side. He didn't meet any resistance on the way. Perhaps it was because he looked so blank and desolate. He passed more traces of violence: broken windows and burnt-out cars. Finally, he was home.

He knocked quietly. His father opened the front door apprehensively. Realising it was his son, he flung it wide and embraced him, burying Lake's face in his armpit. Lake inhaled the familiar smell of lemon aftershave, the same one he'd been wearing for decades. He crumpled in his father's arms.

"Son, you're alive. And your hair!" Lake smiled weakly. His mum pushed past his dad to hug him close to her body. They led him in and shut the world out, double-locking the door behind them and sliding a chain across.

They talked happily at him as he found the couch and sat down heavily, smiling. But Lake felt unable to answer their questions apart from to say he was all right and they didn't need to worry. So instead, they watched him close his eyes and lay his head on the sofa cushions. Very soon, he was in a deep sleep.

He dreamed of a purple mezzanine sky hanging over the inhospitable peaks of Bhutan. The Griffton News tower had been relocated to a mountainside. It was leaning seventy-five degrees to the horizontal. But he couldn't find any people in it, despite searching every floor. All the while, he was running, running. It was an exhausting dream.

He awoke to find a familiar dark-red blanket draped over him and a mug of tea on the table next to him. One of his favourite mugs. Powder-blue anchors on a cream background. His parents were smiling fondly at him.

"How long was I asleep?"

"A few hours," said Blake, his father.

"Hours? How many?"

"Four or five. You can rest all you want to," added his mother, Jemima. "It's no problem. It's just nice to have you back."

"But I've got to get hold of the others," Lake jabbered. Then he made himself relax. "Sorry. How have you two been?" he said, picking up his mug of tea.

"We're okay. Your dad can't go into work anymore, obviously. No one can. We try to stay indoors apart from picking up our rations."

Blake added, "It's all about keeping your head down these days while things get sorted out with the terrorists."

"Oh, I see."

Jemima cut in: "Can we ask you something? Do you have anywhere to stay at the moment? Would you stay here? We'd love to have you with us."

"I would love that. Yeah. The thing is, it didn't work out with the government job. I can't really explain it to you now, but I will soon." Lake fought the tears that swam into his eyes.

"We'd love to have you back, son," agreed Blake.

"All I can say is my life was in danger. It still is."

"You don't need to explain," Jemima smiled. "Home is home and that's all there is to it."

"Thank you. Thank you so much."

"Oh, by the way, a girl called for you. While you were sleeping."

"Rachel? Or was it Kumiko?"

"So many girls," laughed Blake.

Jemima jabbed him gently in the ribs and said, "No. Her name was Iona. She said to give her a call as soon as you can. It sounded urgent. She says you've got her number, but I wrote it down just in case."

Lake sat forward in his chair. "Could I have that number now please?"

Chapter 17

Rory resurfaced from the electric-blue water. He plucked the snorkel out of his mouth and shouted, "This is the coolest thing I've ever done! Even better than the turtles on Turtle Beach!"

He wriggled his body, splashing up water on either side of him. All around him children were bobbing up and down. Some floated face down on the surface. Others kicked down to the depths, returning triumphant. Their high-pitched squeals of delight joined the squawking of the birds overhead.

Earlier that day, they watched the green sea turtles paddle lazily in from the water to bask on the white sandy beach. The creatures were so slow the brothers managed to creep up and stroke them, egged on by their island friends. Rory found the huge shells surprisingly textured beneath his fingertips. They also retained the heat of the sun. Warm to the touch.

Before that, the island kids showed them the old Seventies bowling alley, down near the one and only barber shop. It was still working after all these years, and was a lot tinier than the one back home in Griffton. Rory loved it because they'd painted it bright colours, and each bowling pin was different. The group decided not to have a game today, though, because it was so nice outside.

Rory's new friend Stephen led the way, confidently showing them around Sand Island, spewing out facts and figures. The other kids followed happily, skipping and giggling, ranging in age from preschoolers to teenagers. Bare feet, baggy tee-shirts, straggly hair. The lively gang made up around a third of the people on the island. The older kids stayed with the adults or hung out, doing their own thing.

Stephen proudly informed the Harcourt boys that his island was over one thousand acres in size, and two thousand miles away from the nearest continent. Rory couldn't picture the distance, but it felt to him like the Earth to the Moon: a long, long way from anywhere.

He also learned about the tragedy of plastic contamination. All those thousands of bottles and coloured plastic shrapnel that washed up on the shore each week, destroying the wildlife. The islanders spent much of their time collecting rubbish and helping the birds. He learned that they eat too many scraps of plastic and fall ill or starve. There was little they could actually do for them, which hurt Rory's heart to hear. The birds often died painful, unhappy deaths, he discovered.

They saw the Battle of Midway Monument and wandered up to the Rusty Bucket at the north-western tip. The gentle ice-blue waters tickled the grey rocks there. You could see the ocean stretching out for miles around, like a bright blue duvet. It was also the best vantage point to have a look at the Protector.

The immense angel never moved. He towered above the atoll, rising out of the coral reef like a filmy waterfall. Every time Rory looked up at the incredible creature, his stomach fluttered. The Dunamis had spoken to him yesterday – what an honour. In response, he'd danced on the coral - on the water itself - in front of the King and unlocked the angel. It was the greatest thing he'd ever done in his life. Rory stared at the Protector and beamed, listening to the unending tune that floated through the air high above.

The island's attractions were wonderful. But nothing could beat messing about in the ocean at the very centre of the Pacific. Both Rory and his older brother Cameron quickly learned how to dive down, have a look at the fish, then shoot back up and expel the water from their snorkel tubes. Cameron had done some snorkelling before with Micah, but only on the surface of the sea. Unlike Griffton beach, the waters around Midway Atoll were warm and clear.

Stephen pointed out some truly impressive fish. "This one is a fantail filefish. White with black spots. Sometimes they're yellow with orange tails."

"How about that spotted one? Is that a fantail filefish as well?" asked Rory.

"No. That's a different shape altogether and much smaller. That fellow with the big red eye is a spotted cardinal fish. They are one of my favourites."

"Yeah, they look really friendly. He's like a six-pointed star. I'm going to try and draw him later."

"If we swim out a bit further, I'll show you a Hawaiian grouper. Well, I'll try to. They're pretty rare. Sometimes they swim with the masked angelfish. You're gonna love them!"

Rory and Cameron learned to watch out for the spiky black sea urchins in the shallows. It was something the boys took very seriously after hearing a few cautionary tales of people getting hurt.

"Sea urchins mostly eat algae and rotting stuff, like fish and sponge."

"Really?"

"Absolutely. And did you know you can eat sea urchin? Some people cook them up with onion and lemon juice."

"No way. They look too spiky."

"No, silly. You take all that junk off first."

"Well, it sounds disgusting to me," quipped Cameron.

Stephen replied, "Actually, it is really horrible. Slimy like custard."

After they finished in the water, they sat on the sand, drying quickly under the hot sun. It was their turn to tell the island kids about life in England.

Surrounded by the crowd of local children, Rory described, in great detail, all the different sweets you could get. His audience listened without blinking, imagining the flavours in their mouths: the sweetness, the fizzing or the sourness. The island children didn't have a very good variety of sweets and never had. For them it was a dream. Rory felt sorry for them.

Next, Cameron told them all about Griffton Cliff and its wildlife, as well as the forests to the north, the tall buildings and Eagle Manor Boys' School. But he trailed off as he told them about the lessons and break-time fun, because he started to miss his friends.

The afternoon wore on slowly and became a warm and pleasant evening. Erin, one of the older girls from the village approached them and called them to eat. She had incredibly long black hair and dark eyelashes, Rory noticed. As she wandered up to them, she kicked through the sand slowly with her bare feet, only to find the crowd giggling uncontrollably. To make matters worse, they wouldn't tell her why.

Later on Stephen sheepishly explained to her that, seconds before she arrived, one of the kids had pointed out one of the local birds, shouting out "Hey! There's a Brown Booby!" And then she walked over, so they started giggling. However, Erin wasn't offended and saw the funny side.

They frequently ate together as a community, the eight families and handful of individuals of Sand Island. Each brought a prepared dish and ate outdoors, enjoying each other's company. Music, singing, stories and dances often featured at their gatherings. Tonight, was one of these community meals. It was more than big enough to feed the forty-seven of them plus four guests.

The kids meandered back to the settlement where food was already being brought out, adding coconut and spice aromas to the warm breeze. There were trays of fried fish, fresh vegetables and hot rice.

As soon as Rory caught sight of his parents, he raced over and put his arms around them both. He loved the fact they were getting time together and had their arms around each other. It made him want to sing.

He jabbered about his day. Cameron walked up to join them and added his own details every so often. Daniel and Arabella smiled as the boys talked over each other.

"One at a time, otherwise we can't understand either of you," suggested their father, but not unkindly.

Before long, they were relaxing together and eating, as their parents chatted with Stephen's parents, Judah and Hannah, and some of the others.

Rory got to eat some of his favourite dishes from the island. One of them was deep-fried battered white fish. They ate small chunks of it with a special coconut dip. To accompany this, he had a sweet mixed-fruit smoothie with a yellow straw. Cameron went for the sweet rice with cubes of colourful vegetable. But Rory preferred the choice he'd made. So he didn't ask for any of his brother's, for a change.

Around dessert time, just as Rory was teaching Stephen a few parkour moves, he heard a strange hissing noise in the sky. Looking up, he gasped as he saw a creature from the mezzanine swoop down.

It was an Angel Hunter. Talons, teeth, black leather wings. Diving like a biplane.

Chapter 18

Somebody screamed near him. In seconds, the demon was upon them, trying to snatch Erin. She was standing near the campfire, over by the food tables.

Rory watched it all happen in what seemed like slow motion, his whole body tensing. He saw the creature put its arms out to grab Erin. She shrieked, unable to move. Stephen sprinted over and took hold of her. He flung his arms around her and shielded her with his body. But the monster scooped them both up. Seconds later they were off the ground.

The adults sprinted over to the fire but arrived too late. Stephen and Erin were already high up in the air. Rory could hear her muffled screams above. He looked over to his parents to get a steer on what to do. His Dad wore a stern expression.

"Look! There are more of them," someone called out. Two more dark shapes appeared in the sky. They soared confidently like birds of prey.

"Grab hands!" Judah commanded. "You know what to do, people. Seek the Rescuer with your hearts. Ask the King with your spirits. He is good and he is in charge."

They closed their eyes, bowed their heads and found their place of peace.

"Rescuer King, you got this," said Judah firmly. "You love us and we know you make all things work together for the good of those who love you."

The music in the air intensified as the islanders' faith spurred the Protector on. They saw it shimmer on the far side of the atoll. It wove a string of complex and lovely notes that sounded to Rory like an orchestra playing the sweetest music.

One of the three figures in the sky moved like an arrow. It flew directly at the Angel Hunter who held the two teenagers. The arrow held resolutely to its course. Then, as Rory watched it, with eyes like halogen lamps and his mouth wide open, he saw that it was a Warrior Angel. It was blazing with white fire. Three more bright angels followed it from near the Protector. They ripped through the sky making three chalk-white lines.

The first one reached the Angel Hunter. It swung its long sword in an arc that started behind its back and ended at the thick neck of the beast. But the creature had already dropped Stephen and Erin who were rapidly plummeting towards the deep water.

"Save them!" Rory yelped, without even realising he'd said the words. He instantly remembered being taken by one of these things a few days earlier and lifted high into the air as he ran towards the stone head.

In no time at all, a Warrior Angel rocketed downwards to pluck first one then the other up and bring them safely to shore. He placed them gently down, leaving them standing hand-in-hand on the beach, gazing in wonder. Then he took to the skies to finish the job.

Fierce fighting ensued above their heads as swords and wings clashed. The demonic howls could clearly be heard over the island. Regardless, the community felt a deep peace as the Dunamis poured reassurance into their hearts. The enemy quickly found themselves outnumbered two to one, fighting for their very existence against the six angelic warriors.

They raged at their attackers and snarled at the sound of the Protector's singing which offended their ears so greatly. Roars of agony were forced from their lips as the flaming swords bit into them. Suddenly it was over.

They tumbled helplessly through the air as they departed their leathery bodies: spirit snakes shedding their redundant skins. The carcass shells shattered on impact with the water. They carried on travelling downwards in pieces. Soon to become abandoned detritus on the seabed, ready to decay further. But the core of their demonic beings had already left for the endless punishment beyond. The island was safe again, for the moment.

The Protector's harmonic notes were all that remained: rhythmic and quiet now, washing over Spit, Sand and Eastern Islands. The islanders hugged Erin and Stephen, holding them close, tearful but thankful that nobody was harmed.

The islanders had a lot to talk about that evening. They repeatedly checked on Stephen and Erin. And they quizzed the Harcourt family about their adventures in the mezzanine. They wanted to know everything about the Warrior Angels and the Angel Hunters.

Soon, nightfall arrived. They sat together around the campfire, checking the skies frequently and giving thanks to the Creator all the while.

Judah spoke. "It is the first time this island has seen such evil."

Daniel nodded, looking serious, Rory, Cameron and Arabella sat close by.

"Do you think it's over?" asked Rory.

Judah shook his head. "I wonder if this is happening all over the world? But we have the Protector of the air and we have our faith: we are confident that our hope for a better world will become reality."

"I suspect our time on this island paradise will soon be over," noted Daniel. Rory thought his father looked sad.

"But how do we get home, Dad?" Cameron enquired. "We're in the middle of the sea, miles from anywhere. We might as well be on Mars."

Arabella said, "If angels can appear in the sky, then surely we can get back to Griffton." She smiled.

"Well, we only need four of them," Rory observed. "One for me, one for Cam and you two."

"How fast do you think they can fly?" asked his brother.

"I don't know. Let's ask them." Daniel headed off towards the beach where the six angels had just landed.

Chapter 19

Serena sat up in her borrowed bed. Her eyes were open but she didn't see the room around her. She saw a cliff instead. The big, broad structure at the top of the city. The thing they called Griffton Cliff. She'd been there before, she remembered. They'd exited the stone head, looking for the Malkin. The city lay beneath them, down in the valley.

In her head, it was dusk. Crowds of people gathered. They knelt in concentric circles. A multitude of people, their clothes tatty and covered with the dust of fallen buildings. Grey mist swirled around them. It was the mist of the enemy, not the Creator. Pinpoints of light sparkled within, mesmerising anyone who looked at them. Samyaza was there. She could feel the burden of his presence.

Then Serena heard chanting, low and guttural. It rose and fell, the voices sounding in unison. The people were giving their worship to Samyaza. They were giving him glory as their king. She shuddered.

In the midst of the crowd was the focus of their attention. The stone statue of Samyaza towered above their heads. Though the rocky cliff rose high above Griffton, it was overshadowed by the statue of the dark angel with its wings aloft. It measured thirty metres - a hundred feet - from its base to the top of its head. Its wingspan made it almost twice as broad as it was high, forming the shape of a massive plus sign.

She was unable to look at its face. Her spirit prevented her. But she knew its expression and it was something she did not want to see. Repulsive waves of evil came at her. All the while, the voices chanted.

Serena came out of the vision and the room formed around her. She was back in the present. It hadn't happened yet. Or was it happening now? Surely there was still time? Time to do something.

"Caleb, we have to stop him," she said.

Already wide awake, and gazing at her with a concerned expression, Caleb said, "Tell me everything."

"We've seen some terrible things, my darling Caleb. Here and in the other place. And I know we're going to see even more. I feel there is something new coming. On the cliff. They'll set it on the cliff. And people will be forced to go there and bow down. And they will do it. And then they'll be lost forever. Their hearts will die."

"A statue?"

Serena nodded, waves of blonde hair falling across her shiny green eyes. She brushed them back.

"We knew this a long time ago. We knew it would come," said Caleb quietly.

They heard the sound of glass breaking downstairs.

"Did you check all the rooms?" Serena whispered.

"Yes. The house was empty. I felt the Dunamis lead us here. The owners will not return."

They listened hard. Sounds of movement. Quiet steps, almost imperceptible.

"Micah?"

"I don't think so. He said he'd go for an early morning walk this morning. And he'd whistle when he came back."

"What then? The enemy?"

"I'm going down."

"Caleb, be careful."

He tiptoed carefully down the stairs. The corner step creaked

87

horribly. Caleb frowned at it. Crisp morning sunlight illuminated the stairwell. Concentrating hard, Caleb peered as far as he could, his fists raised.

In the kitchen, he saw the intruder. The mysterious arrival was a furry cat with a perfectly-spherical head and a long tail. The creature scampered backwards. Caleb noted the broken bottle near the kitchen counter.

"It's all right," he reassured it, soothingly. Backing away, he called up the stairs, "A cat, Serena. It's just a hungry cat."

"Oh, that's a relief," Serena called down.

Moving slowly, Caleb looked around for something to feed it. The fruit in the fruit bowl was rotten and gave off an unpleasant smell. But he found some milk in the fridge which seemed acceptable. He poured it into a bowl, placing it down near the cat.

Tentatively, it trod forward, sniffing. It was a long-haired grey cat with a crimson collar. Somebody's pet. Perhaps it belonged to the absent owners.

As the cat happily finished off the milk, Caleb checked the whole of the downstairs, just in case. Everything seemed to be in order.

"Would you like me to bring you a coffee, Serena?" he called up the stairs. "They've got milk."

"Yes, that would be lovely darling. But I'm just going to have a wash first and then I'll come down and drink it with you. Give me fifteen minutes."

When Micah appeared, whistling a cheery tune at the front door, Serena was finishing off her coffee. She held the lemon-yellow mug close to her face. It belonged to the lady of the house. She knew this with prophetic certainty, and also that the homeowners had died in a building collapse. They weren't coming back.

Caleb opened the front door to a fresh breeze and Micah in a cadmium-blue hoodie, carrying a crusty baguette. Bright, almond-shaped eyes smiled at him.

"Hi Caleb. I brought breakfast. Hungry?"

"Great timing," grinned Caleb. "Yes, famished."

Caleb looked up and down the street in this west Griffton suburb. Nobody was about. Micah wandered in.

"Much happening out there?" asked Serena.

"It's really strange. After all the drama in Tanzania with Ndege and the Protector of the Land. Then our crazy trip back through the mezzanine. That was really wild by the way. After all that, it seems very quiet in Griffton. Not what I expected at all. I thought there'd be chaos everywhere."

"Good to know you can still get fresh bread," she observed.

"There was this bakery that opened out onto the street. Even the Dream Fighters were buying breakfast. I talked to the man, and he said business is good."

"I guess if you've got the support of the enemy, business is bound to be good," Caleb noted. "Did you learn anything else?"

"People weren't really talking much. They all seemed to mind their own business. I walked past a lot of smashed up buildings. There's definitely a war going on here. And the people know it. So what's the plan Caleb?"

"We finish up here, make some sandwiches and head on out. Let's make a difference out there."

Serena started to frown. "What is it, my love?" asked Caleb.

"I have a strong sense that Rachel is in danger. She's all alone. And we can't reach her." Tears formed in her eyes. "But the Rescuer is by her side."

"We should go to Eddie's house next. See if she's there," Caleb declared. The other two nodded.

Then they left their temporary home behind. Serena was thankful for her sleep and shower, freezing though it was. They picked up their backpacks – the same ones they'd had since they'd entered the mezzanine from Griffton Cliff. To Serena it seemed a very long time ago.

Since then, they'd hiked on foot through the foreboding caves and encountered the violent shape shifter, Zed, who tried to murder them. They had crossed a broad lake on their home-made raft and re-entered their home-world in Tanzania. Seeing Ndege healed, and watching the Protector of the land rise up, caused their spirits to soar. It made the whole adventure worthwhile, with its ups and downs, thought Serena.

Then came the arduous journey back to Griffton, tumbling in and out of the mezzanine, led by angels. It was a blur now, but pieces of it swam before her eyes. The thrilling heat of Africa. The red rocks. A short journey on an ocean liner. Black demons swooping down. Wine-red mountains. White earthly mountains. A brief flight through the mezzanine along with the pterodactyls. The salty aroma of the sea. Long green grass. Urban grey: the glassy upsweep of skyscrapers. And sleep. That's how they had come to settle in this west Griffton house, led by the Dunamis, protected by angels, while chaos spun around them.

On leaving the house, it wasn't long before their help was needed. They moved from a residential area to a built-up business district. Unusually, it was devoid of activity. There were no commuter cars or delivery vans on the road. No suited workers entered or left the offices.

A compact, standalone building drew their attention. Although it was intact on the outside, its insides had collapsed. Looking through the glass windows was rather like looking at an hourglass that had run out of time. There was a mound of monochrome debris at the centre of the office space where the ceiling had fallen in. The rubble rose to a point.

Both Serena and Caleb stopped in their tracks at the same time. They looked at each other, and then looked around to see what the Dunamis was telling them.

"Somebody's under all that," whispered Serena. Caleb immediately agreed.

In seconds, they were shovelling through the dirt: stone, wood, paint and plaster.

Chapter 20

Choking on the dusty stench, Micah spotted a woman's black patent leather shoe. Sombrely, he pointed it out to the others. Arms already filthy, he dove further into the huge pile of waste. Working together on their hands and knees, they found their prize: an older woman who was alive but unconscious. She was bleeding in several places.

It took a huge effort to shift furniture and chunks of masonry away. But they eventually freed her. Caleb carefully carried her over to a clear part of the oatmeal carpet and laid her down gently. Meanwhile, Micah searched frantically for other people but didn't find anyone else.

They gathered around the woman. Her hair was either white or so thick with dust that it looked colourless. Then they closed their eyes, knowing instinctively what to do.

"Sweet Dunamis," breathed Serena. "Bring her back won't you?" She stared at the woman, smiling sadly, knowing the Dunamis was fully capable of doing this but that it might not be his plan. Peace fell on the three of them as they waited.

The injured woman groaned and opened her eyes. "Who are you?" she croaked. Her eyes moved slowly from Serena to Caleb to Micah, then settled back on Serena's tender countenance.

Serena beamed into her face and said gently, "We are your friends, precious one. And you are alive. Very much alive. Now, can you tell us where it hurts?"

She had a quiet, low voice. "Friends? Thank you. My leg. Right leg. My arms, all the way up. And my ribs." Tears streamed from her eyes, carving tracks down her dusty cheeks.

"Okay. Rest up a minute and we're going to ask the Rescuer to heal you through his Dunamis. Is that all right?"

The woman gasped. "The Rescuer. But he's bad, isn't he?" She widened her eyes as though expecting a slap.

"You can be the judge of that. Would you like to be healed?"

"Yes," she said quietly, and then lay still.

Serena closed her eyes. "Gentle Rescuer, mighty Dunamis, and Creator of all things, would you make this woman well again? Please show her your unfailing love for her. Let her know how special she is to you. Take away her pain and give her your strength."

Nothing happened for a while, and then everything happened at once. Her broken ribs and the bones in her arms shifted back into place and became like new. The pain departed from her arms and neck. Power pulsed through her body. She squealed with delight and sat up, invigorated. "How did you do that?" Her voice was stronger than before.

"Would you like to know?" Caleb asked, looking her squarely in the face.

The woman stared back at him, deadly serious. "Yes. I believe you owe me an explanation, young man."

"Well, to start with, it wasn't us. There's no healing power that comes from me. But the Rescuer loves you, lady, and wants you to know how much. He's the one who healed you. Would you like to know him?"

"Of course," she shot back.

°°°°°12345°°°°°

Her name was Belle Clancy. They reunited her with her daughter Jennie and her husband Alejandro. who lived on the eastern side of town. Belle was brimming over with joy and eager to tell everybody about the Rescuer and his Dunamis, regardless of the trouble it might cause her.

"If you are sure, then we will be on our way," said Caleb at the door.

"I can't thank you enough for what you've done," said the woman, giving Serena one last hug.

"In that case, it's à bientôt - until we meet again," Caleb smiled.

Hearing her excited voice trail away behind them, they walked on, in search of Russet Road. Caleb felt confident it was nearby, but followed prompts from the Dunamis nonetheless.

They travelled through a little park with a children's roundabout and a small line of broken swings. It led to an unremarkable row of houses. Terraced. Uniform. Nothing special.

"Ah, yes. This looks familiar," murmured Caleb. They noted the street sign for Russet Road and followed the line as the house numbers increased two at a time.

"That's number thirty, so forty-two Russet Road must be just a bit further," noted Micah. "Let's hope Rachel and Eddie are home, and they've got the kettle on for us."

The houses were grey and tired-looking. The smell of bonfires hung in the air, but, in reality, much of Griffton now carried that aroma. Very soon, they reached their destination. It was starkly illuminated by the bright morning sun.

"Oh no," uttered Serena. "I don't believe it. Rachel!"

The three of them ground to a halt in front of Eddie's house, or what was left of it. Although it was still standing, huge black tendrils of soot reached from the ground up to the top of the wall where the roof used to be. Fire-damaged beyond repair, the empty building stood forlorn and useless.

They stood silently for a while, lost in their own thoughts. Then Serena said, "She's not in there. And nor is Eddie. Nobody's inside."

Just to confirm it, a voice behind them asked, "Are you friends of Eddie?"

Caleb turned slowly around and saw an older man wearing

brown slip-on shoes with formal trousers and a cornflower-blue shirt with big collars.

"Yes, we are," Caleb answered warily.

"We're so sorry about the house. It was the girl. The one on the telly. She did it. I would have stopped them but there were too many and they had guns. Eddie's going to be so upset when he finds out. He's away right now. I'm Corbyn by the way. I live opposite."

"Pleased to meet you, Corbyn."

"I've known him for years. I would have stopped them you know. If I was younger. It's not right what they did. They are not good people."

"No. They're not."

"Not that you can say anything about it. It's not allowed." He looked up and down the street quickly, scanning for Dream Fighters. And then he whispered, "But if you ask me, I think they made up this terrorist threat so they could get into power. It wouldn't be the first time in human history. Irene agrees with me. She's my wife."

Serena smiled at him and said in her soft Californian tones, "I would just love a cup of tea. We've travelled a very long way. Do you have any to spare?"

"Yes of course. Any friends of Eddie's are friends of ours. Why don't you come into the house? Irene, would love to meet you, I'm sure."

Chapter 21

"You're gonna give us your watch, your mobile, your wallet and any jewellery she has on her," demanded the man. "And if you don't, we'll kill the kids."

Rory watched everything unfold in minute detail. From the mud on the man's boots to the tone of his voice, he took it all in. His senses were alive. What were those smells? Tobacco. Petrol. Leather.

He'd seen stuff like this before on telly. Someone usually stopped the baddies, particularly in the movies aimed at kids. But he knew real life was different. There was no way of knowing how this might go.

He tried not to look scared. He'd already seen a lot of destruction on the way up from Griffton beach. There were a lot of burnt out cars and smashed windows. No one had cleared up. It looked a bit like the TV pictures after a tsunami or hurricane had passed through.

The city was completely different from how he remembered it. He'd been asleep when his angel had flown across France with him. But he started to wake up over the English Channel. Even though the air was cold up there, the angel kept him warm somehow. Heat came out of his body, like he was a big hot water bottle. And what he saw beneath him as they descended into Griffton was like a dream. A bad dream.

Some of the buildings had been knocked down flat. There was a lot of smoke and fire across the city. It reminded him of one of his war games. Or maybe a movie set that was filming an adventure at the end of the world. As they came into land, he remembered looking across to Cameron whose face showed the horror he felt. They both knew Griffton had changed forever.

And then the angels set them down on the beach and disappeared. The family hugged each other then wandered up to the city. They went in search of breakfast because Rory and Cameron were famished. And that's when they bumped into these bad men, in the winding streets. They were just looking for some toast and eggs but instead they found these guys, Rory recalled.

His father made himself tall and shoved him and Cameron behind him with one arm. Dad was a hero, thought Rory, as he waited to see what he would do next.

"Listen, I don't want you to get hurt," said Daniel in a low growl to their two attackers. They scoffed at this. One of them held a knife, the other a sharp metal pole.

"Funny man," said the shorter of the two who had wild, red hair.

"So, are you going to hurt us then?" asked the other, who had a scratchy voice and a shaved head. He winked at his friend.

"Oh no, not me. I mean, I could if I wanted to. No. It isn't me you need to worry about. It's those guys you really don't want to mess with," said Daniel, nodding over behind them.

The muggers turned around slowly, still holding their weapons. They stared as they realised they were hemmed in by two Warrior Angels. The beings stood twelve feet tall from top to bottom. Electric currents of white light travelled up and down their long, drawn swords and across their dazzling robes. Their expressions were set: stern and unimpressed. To Rory, they looked like smaller versions of the massive Protector on the island. The shaven-headed man turned back to Daniel, mouth agape.

Daniel commented, "You have a choice you know. You always have a choice. My friend Caleb taught me that. And it starts with laying down your arms. Just put them slowly on the ground.

Nobody needs to get hurt. After that, it can go a couple of ways. The great thing is, you get to decide."

The men did what he asked and put down the knife and pole.

"I used to be like you, you know."

"No you didn't," said the man with red hair.

"Oh, that's where you're wrong. I enjoyed hurting people. Loved it. When I was younger, I'd just do it for kicks. But there is another way to live. A better way. If you carry on your way, you might get what you want, whenever you want. But there's a price to pay. The one I work for, the King of this world, he's your boss too, whether you like it or not. And he will hold you to account for what you do and what you've done."

"You're one of those Rescuer people, aren't you?" spat the man.

"Yes. We are friends of the Rescuer. And so are these two behind you."

"I don't want anything to do with all that," said the shaven-headed man. "I'm not a goody-goody loser and I never want to be. Kill us or let us go. We don't care."

But the other man said quietly, "What do you mean he's the King of the world? We heard Samyaza's the only one in charge and this Rescuer's an impostor. A troublemaker."

"So, why aren't you following him instead - if he's such a troublemaker?"

"We don't follow anyone."

"But you just said Samyaza is the one in charge."

"Yes. But I don't follow anyone."

"But you follow him, right?"

"You're confusing me," said the red-headed man. "Putting words in my mouth."

Far away, the Protectors of the Land, Sea and Air were singing, now fully activated. They were stationed in Bhutan, Tanzania and Midway Atoll. Ideally positioned to cover the whole earth. And they were glorious. Flashes of lightning sparked across their mountainous forms. Enormous, filmy wings stretched out. Their preternatural music flowed across the surface of the globe and entered the space between the spaces.

And, though human ears were unable to discern it, they called people by name tenderly, lovingly. Knocking softly on the doors of their hearts. Looking for souls who were open to their song. The song of the Rescuer.

The Protector of the Sea sang the name "Pete". "Vince" sang the Land Protector. Rotating through the names of the living, they called persistently, caressing the people's hearts with their melodies, looking for an open door.

"We can settle this right now," Daniel said. "You can ask the Rescuer himself if you want. Ask him to let you know who he really is."

"No way, man. This is a trick," said the taller of the two. Suddenly, he bolted away from the Warrior Angels and his friend and ran for freedom. Dodging past Rory and his family, he was gone in seconds. Rory was secretly pleased and relaxed a little.

Daniel turned back to the redheaded man, noting that the guardian angels had vanished. However, the strong presence of the Dunamis bathed them with his peace.

"What's your name, friend," he asked kindly.

"Pete. It's Pete Carrington."

"I'm Daniel. Sit with us a while?" They sat on the curb. Rory and Cameron looked on with huge eyes.

Daniel asked, "Tell me something, Pete. Is this really who you are? Is this who you want to be? In your heart of hearts?"

Arabella smiled sweetly at him by Daniel's side and put her hand on the man's arm. She waited patiently.

After thinking for a while, he admitted, "No. It's not. I was a painter decorator before everything changed. I was really good at it. That's who I am. Vince, my friend, he had a web business fixing electronics for people. But you know, desperate times..."

"We understand," said Arabella.

"They've done a number on you," said Daniel.

"Come again?"

"Samyaza and these Dream Fighters. They're charging around

98

like they own the place. But all they're doing is causing carnage. He wants everyone to bow the knee to him. Give him their lives. It's because he hates the Creator, the Rescuer and their Dunamis and the people they created. But in the end, when Samyaza doesn't get his way, he'll just kill everyone, one way or another. Believe me, I used to be like you." Daniel sighed deeply.

"So what's the answer?" Pete enquired. His eyes were wide open.

"Follow the Rescuer - put your trust in him. He loves you, man."

"That's what you've done, right? All of you? Even the kids? Is that why the angels came to look after you?"

"Yes, that's right," said Arabella.

"So what do I do?"

Rory piped up, "It's easy! You do it from your heart and you do it by believing. Believing in the Rescuer." He grinned.

Daniel elaborated, "You turn away from all the bad stuff you've done. Tell the Rescuer you're sorry. Grab his forgiveness. You walk free from the bad stuff that's been done to you - forgive. And you give your life over to him, put him in charge from now on. It really is as simple as that. Just like my boy said."

Arabella added, "You want to make your peace with the Creator, don't you? That's what your heart is telling you. I can sense it."

Pete stared at the ground. "Yeah. I'd like that."

Daniel continued, "Then, if you're willing, the Rescuer's Dunamis will come and live in you. He'll speak to you and help you. Then, whether you live or die, you'll be free of Samyaza forever. And you'll be with the Rescuer forever in a place where there is no more death or sadness or pain."

"Live or die?"

"Absolutely," Daniel confirmed. "He loves you, brother. It's what he wants. He has great things for you."

"Okay. I'm ready," Pete looked at them expectantly. "Let's do this thing. You've got the angels on your side. I need some of that myself. I want what you've got."

Chapter 22

Pete walked away a changed man. His perspective on life altered completely. He was eager to find Vince and tell him. He couldn't thank the family enough. Daniel settled for directions to the best breakfast he could think of.

It was a tiny cafe in west central Griffton, in what used to be someone's front room. Floral tablecloths covered half a dozen round tables, brightening the place with yellows, reds and orange hues.

The place was empty apart from the owner, a long and lanky man with a grey moustache and sad eyes. He sat slumped in a chair but jumped up when the Harcourt family entered. His face transformed as they enquired about a table.

"You want to eat?" he sounded surprised but delighted. It was almost as though he'd forgotten what customers looked like. He welcomed them warmly and waved his long fingers about as he showed them to a table.

Arabella and Daniel sat down heavily and looked at the menus as the boys went in search of a toilet. As soon as they returned, the owner was back at their table and in full flow, talking them through the menu.

"I can offer you hot, home-baked bread, which is delicious. And I have eggs - scrambled, fried, poached or omelettes and also baked beans. Sorry, we don't have that or that. I'm sure you understand, the times being what they are. But to drink I have orange and apple juice, black tea or coffee. No milk, sorry, just powdered."

"Sounds very good to us," said Arabella.

"I feel I must apologise that we don't have any of the usual things you'd find in a full English breakfast: sausages, bacon, tomatoes or mushrooms. Such a shame. Before the troubles started, I had all of these things in the kitchen. But not anymore."

"That's fine, really. We're easy to please."

The boys were delighted to hear that he did have tomato ketchup, however. Lots of it. For them, that would suffice for vegetables.

When the food arrived, Rory's smile stretched right across his face. He wriggled in his seat. A cloud of breakfast smells filled the modest diner.

"Feels like we haven't eaten in days," he sighed, before demolishing his hot breakfast.

"Surely you ate enough for a week on the island?" asked Daniel, sipping his black coffee. "All that fresh fish and coconut rice."

"Nah," Rory grinned.

The owner left them alone while they ate. There was nobody else to bother them, which was nice. Only a couple of people walked past the cafe, Rory noticed. To him, it felt like a sanctuary: a safe harbour from the upheaval outside. If he had his way, they'd stay there all day, drinking orange juice and eating soft-boiled eggs with toast soldiers. That was his favourite. Cameron, on the other hand, preferred fried eggs, toast and Marmite, but nobody was allowed to cut up his toast. It had to be one big square because that's how he liked it. And no butter.

"So, what's next darling?" Arabella asked Daniel.

"Find the others if we can. Maybe they've come back here as well. No one's replying to my messages. Maybe their mobiles aren't working, or maybe they're still out of the country."

"I know Caleb doesn't have a mobile phone. He doesn't like them," Arabella commented. "How about Lytescote?"

"Yes, we could try to check on the house if we can, though

it might be too dangerous. My inclination is that we check on Eddie and Rachel's house first. I'm sure it isn't far from here. We are already on the west side as it is."

"Hey, it's a plan!" said Rory, and pulled a cheeky face. Daniel put his face right up close to his son's, stared at him for a minute and then quacked like a duck. Rory gasped and tittered and Cameron did his big laugh.

"Oh dad, you're so silly," said Rory.

Griffton was quiet, but there were more people on the streets now. They walked purposefully, avoiding each other's gaze and looking busy. Policing the streets here and there were pairs of Dream Fighters. Daniel kept his head down, holding hands with Arabella and Rory. Nobody stopped them.

He was right, Eddie's house was not far at all. It was a shock to all of them when they found it in ruins.

Rory burst into tears as soon as he caught sight of it. Cameron stared soberly and Arabella rushed towards the wreckage looking for signs of life.

"No, Bella. This fire's been out for a long time. If there is anyone under there, they're not going to be alive."

Arabella's eyes had pain in them as she looked back at her husband. "Oh, Dan, no," she whispered.

Chapter 23

The inside of Rory's head felt like rushing wind. That's the only way he could describe it. He tried to imagine what it all meant, the burned-down house in front of him. Could it mean his new friends, Rachel and Eddie, were under the sludgy rubble? The thought filled his whole mind. It was hard to think about anything else. He saw a bright blue plastic corner sticking up out of a pile of bricks. Cameron fidgeted beside him.

Then suddenly, they were overwhelmed by people. Somebody put an arm around him. He turned and saw it was Micah. Meanwhile, a tough guy with short white hair was giving his dad a hug: Caleb Noble. He recognised them instantly.

"Micah! And Caleb!" he shouted. "Is it really you?"

Daniel, Arabella and the boys suddenly found themselves being embraced by their good friends, Caleb, Micah and Serena. Another man, whom Rory didn't recognise, smiled shyly and stood aloof next to a woman. They were both wearing matching grey jumpers.

"We saw you all from the window. We live over there," said the man in the jumper, pointing to the house opposite. "We do have more tea. You must come inside."

The friends took turns hugging each other again. Rory's heart swelled with joy as everyone cooed and fussed. It felt to him like a street party. The ruined building behind them faded instantly from his mind.

"Did you manage to do it?" asked Daniel. "Did you?"

Caleb's face beamed back at him. "We did. It was amazing. Beautiful. We made it to Tanzania and got help from a local boy. He knew the Dunamis."

Daniel shot back: "Caleb. I've never seen anything like it in my life. Ours was massive. It towered over the island. And the sound it made. Unreal! Beyond words." Caleb nodded. "We found a whole community of people who follow the Rescuer. Who'd have thought? On an island in the middle of the ocean!" continued Daniel.

Meanwhile, Rory was telling Micah all about Midway Atoll. He described how he was the one to activate the Protector. How they made lots of new friends. And all the amazing food they ate. And the turtles and the bowling alley. And they got to go snorkelling and meet angels. Only not in the mezzanine – in the actual real world. Micah listened hard, grinning all the while.

Daniel became sombre, "Rachel?" he asked pointedly. Caleb looked serious and Serena shook her head. "The truth is we don't know. But, like you, we sense something's wrong."

Micah added, "We tried calling them all. Rachel, Eddie and Lake. Can't get hold of any of them. The phone network's a mess." He shrugged. "No idea if they made it to the mountains. Or if they did their bit. No idea."

The shy man stepped forward. "Excuse me. You are welcome to come inside," he said quietly. "It's not safe out here and we live just over there. I'm Corbyn Burrows and this is my wife Irene. Come in, will you? Our front room isn't very big but we do have tea."

Looking up and down the road, Mr and Mrs Burrows ushered their guests into the house quickly and efficiently.

Once inside, the seven travellers filled the living room, just as they'd filled Eddie's house before their journey through the mezzanine. Rory remembered to take his shoes off and put them by the door. He made sure Cameron did the same.

For Rory, entering the house was like stepping back through time. It felt like he was walking into an old movie. Or one of those old houses where they preserved furniture from the past. Pastel pink sofas rested on ornate wooden feet. The couches had white lace doilies where your head went. Faded seaside pictures and watercolours of ships and birds hung in the middle of the walls in the hall and front room. There was a sweet and musky odour that wasn't unpleasant. It was just old, felt Rory. He'd encountered a similar thing when they first explored Lytescote Manor.

He was so glad to see Micah again. It was like he'd got his older brother back. He played with Micah's hands, prodding and slapping them. At the same time, he showered him with questions about his journey and adventures. Micah stayed calm as an oak tree, as he always did. He gave clear answers about their route through the mezzanine, the wild animals and the Ngorongoro crater. Both Rory and Cameron wanted to know everything.

Soon, Rory was allowed a special can of fizzy blackcurrant drink. Cameron looked unhappy until he was given one too. The cans gave a satisfying hiss as they clicked the metal tabs open. They were super careful opening their drinks so as not to spill anything on Mr and Mrs Burrows' carpet.

After that, Arabella made polite small talk with Irene, asking if she and her husband had seen Eddie or Rachel recently. Corbyn said he approached Eddie to do some small electrical and plumbing jobs. It emerged that it had been a while, and they were the last people to see them in the mezzanine. The conversation came to a natural pause.

"So, Corbyn and Irene," said Daniel firmly, and with some urgency. "Has Caleb asked you the question yet?"

The man looked nonplussed and raised his eyebrows.

"Where are you at with the Rescuer? Are you with the Dream Fighters and their master, Samyaza? Or have you made your decision for the Rescuer? There are only two sides in this fight. Stay on the fence and you'll fall off, and the enemy will pick you off because he doesn't play fair."

Daniel added firmly, "The thing is, the Rescuer, he loves you so much, brother. And Samyaza really does not. In fact he only wants to do you harm. Trust me, I know."

Corbyn stared at him a moment. "I don't know. But what I do know is that we are definitely not with them." He paused to think. "The people in charge are liars. You can't trust them. That's for certain. They got there by force. I don't agree with their tactics. And I saw the young girl burn down Eddie's house with her gang. I saw them do it with my own eyes. It's terrible what they're doing. But what can we do?"

Caleb nodded. He said in a strong voice, "We live in dangerous times. Perhaps the final days. There is no longer any middle ground. There's no fence to sit on, like Daniel says, because the days are evil. Wouldn't you agree?"

Their host nodded. "So, Corbyn, Irene, are you ready to make your decision; to make your peace with the Creator? He's the one your heart tells you about. I'm right, aren't I? Good. Are you ready to meet the Rescuer's Dunamis?"

The Protectors' tune weaved through the air, unheard by human ears. It travelled down from the mountains, from the island, and from the African crater. The sweet presence of the Dunamis rested on the older couple. It was like a heavy dew on the morning fields. Like honey coating a teaspoon. As they stood there, it breathed life over them: spiritual life, wooing them to open their hearts.

"Yes," Corbyn caught his wife's eye. "Yes, I believe we are. We've been having dreams about him, the King, you know. He's dressed in white. His eyes shine and his hair's made of light." He looked into the distance and Rory grinned, taking everything in.

Finally, Corbyn said, "So, tell us, who is the Rescuer? We need to know. How do we get to know him? Tell us now, we're ready. Tea can wait."

Chapter 24

After their audience with the Dunamis, the couple sat side-by-side on their pink sofa. It seemed to Rory that they glowed, like his luminous putty. When his dad bought it for him, for his last birthday, he told him, "You put it in the sun or under your table lamp so it can soak in the rays. Then it's ready to glow." Rory liked his dad's pun: "ready to go, ready to glow".

Corbyn and Irene had been ready to glow. Now, it was like there was a light inside them and nothing could put it out.

Serena was speaking encouraging words to them, given to her by the Dunamis. Irene smiled, nodded and cried every so often. Her husband was relaxed and very peaceful. Caleb took over from Serena and said he needed to explain some important things to them.

Rory wanted to hear what they were, but his mum led him, Cameron and Micah into the kitchen to give the others some space.

"It's a rather small house," she whispered as they followed the hallway to the back. They discovered the kitchen there. And more pictures of ships and beaches, accompanied by portraits of family members.

Just like the living room, the kitchen was also fascinating. It had a strong scent of cottage flowers and washing-up liquid. Rory spotted a meat slicer, like the one they used on the deli counter at the supermarket. Cameron nudged him and showed him an old-fashioned hand grinder.

"It must be for grinding out flour to make bread," he declared.

"No, I reckon it's for making pasta," Rory insisted.

"I'm not so sure about that," replied the older brother.

There were a couple of wooden chairs, which the boys were allowed to sit on. Rory swung his legs about and took in a row of china plates high up on the kitchen wall. They were decorated with blue pictures and handwriting. Everything was neat and clean. No dirty dishes in the sink.

The window looked out onto a small rectangular patch of grass with colourful flowery borders on three sides. There were two aubergine-coloured garden chairs at the end, facing towards the house, accompanied by a small wooden table. Rory spied a small dog sleeping in the garden: a golden retriever puppy with straw-coloured fur.

Suddenly, two giant Dream Fighter soldiers exploded onto the scene. Rory let out a scream. They stared intensely through the kitchen window. One was a man and one a woman. They both had stern expressions.

At almost the same time, they heard a thunderous knocking at the front door. The kitchen door smashed open. The attackers forced their way in and pressed them back into the hall.

"Move," said the woman gruffly. Both figures wore leather armour and Rory recognised them as being the same enemy gang that had ransacked their house and chased them along Griffton Cliff. The only thing that had saved them was their escape through the stone head.

Arabella took his hand and pulled him close into her body. Micah stood between Cameron and the encroaching Dream Fighters. Rory looked back at Cameron whose lips were pressed tightly together.

Two more heavily-armed warriors stood in the doorway at the front of the house. But Caleb physically blocked their entrance. Behind him, Corbyn and Irene sat and cowered, flanked by Daniel and Serena.

"Everybody out," commanded a soldier at the door. Rory could hear a commotion in the street. There were muted yelps and the sound of footsteps.

"We're staying right here," Caleb stated.

The leading Dream Fighter went for his gun. Rory saw his dad move forward to protect Caleb, but Caleb restrained him with his palm.

Then Rory watched as Caleb closed his eyes, bowed his head and clutched his left wrist with his right palm. His arms limp, he stood perfectly still. Seconds later, the Dream Fighters lay crumpled on the floor. It was over.

Rory looked around him. It was like Caleb had flipped a switch and turned off their power. He looked to his dad for direction. But his dad was looking to Caleb. Time ran twice as slow as normal, like the moment just before you jump off the diving board.

Then Caleb barked, "Right. We'd better move fast. Looks like they're taking everyone into the street. Dunamis? What do we do?"

But it was too late to do anything else. Dream Fighters started streaming into the house. It was like when you overfill a glass but keep pouring anyway, Rory observed. That kind of thing usually got him into trouble with mum. He froze and stared as the men kept coming into the room. Soon, the group was completely surrounded.

A scuffle immediately broke out. Micah started it and was struck with the butt of a weapon. Caleb intervened and got tasered. Rory covered his eyes. A moan escaped from his lips. He felt like he couldn't breathe. Everything was going wrong. However, the power of the Dunamis fell on Caleb and blocked the electric shockwaves as they tried to enter his muscular chest. Rory peeped through his fingers. Caleb looked just fine. He nodded silently to Rory.

Next, they were herded into the street. Caleb went peacefully, led out by two bulky guards.

"You be careful with my husband," yelled Serena.

Rory lost sight of his parents momentarily. Panic scaled his chest. As he left, he saw the Dream Fighters trying to revive the men who were lying on the doorstep. One of them got his cheeks slapped repeatedly, which Rory thought was a little harsh. But the man did open his eyes. This made his comrade grunt and then move on to the next soldier. Rory and the others were pushed along.

Outside, he saw the soldiers bringing more people out and making them stand in the middle of Russet Road. There weren't any cars driving down it, fortunately. There was a huge commotion out there. Neighbours embraced each other. Some cried or complained to the soldiers. The Dream Fighters offered no explanation, brandishing their weapons and pushing people together instead.

Looking down the road, Rory saw clumps of people stretching into the distance. The locals stood at the centre. Guards dotted the pavement on either side. They looked like a string of dark leather towers. His parents and Micah banded together around him and Cameron. His dad looked fierce and determined. Defiant.

"Caleb?" enquired Daniel, searching his friend's face. "Do we act?" Caleb put his lips together and shook his head slowly.

"Not right now. The Rescuer knows," he said in reply.

There was a great commotion above them. Rory looked up to see a sky awash with movement. Flying figures. Fighting figures. Wheeling and clashing. Warrior Angels and Angel Hunters: unmistakable. They'd jumped out of the mezzanine and right into his world. The sky was full of them, executing their aerial acrobatics. Diving dangerously. Soaring triumphantly. Swords clashing against talons and teeth. The din demanded attention and forced people to stop and stare.

Rory tapped Cameron in the ribs with the back of his hand, pointing up with the other. His mouth gaped open.

"I know, Rory! I know!" said Cameron.

Chapter 25

"Where are they taking us?" Rory complained sulkily.

"I don't know, my boy," replied Daniel.

The Dream Fighters started to lead them along Russet Road. Nobody physically resisted. They saw what happened to rebels and how they were dragged out of their houses and unceremoniously dumped in the road like sacks of washing. The brave ones asked where they were being taken. Their questions were met with silence. If anyone tried to engage with the guards, they were told to keep moving. It was worse than school assemblies, thought Rory. Far worse.

A light grey canopy of clouds was forming high up in the sky. A camera-lens filter, designed to fog out the world. It had a draining effect on the colours below. The curb-side grass went from green to grey, and red-brick houses faded to a dull red. A cool breeze blew through the crowd.

The Harcourts stayed in a tight group by holding hands firmly with each other, Daniel, Arabella, Micah, Cameron and Rory. Glued together like this, they stuck close to Serena and Caleb, who seemed absolutely fine. Rory wondered how much it hurt to be tasered. It wasn't something he wanted to experience. His brother had given him a static-electricity shock on his cheek once, which had pinched like a bee sting. That was enough for him to know that electric shocks were not pleasant. But Caleb seemed just fine: his normal self, which was a relief.

Unfortunately, their new friends fell back and it wasn't possible to be reunited. The guards demanded everyone kept flowing forwards rather than straggling backwards. If anyone went the wrong way, the Dream Fighters screamed and roared or shoved them with a heavy hand or the butt of a gun.

Before they lost them, Caleb managed to call out, "Corbyn, trust him and do not be afraid. He knows all things and he is ultimately in charge. You know that, right?" Corbyn nodded shyly.

"Good then. We'll see you on the other side." Caleb beamed at his new friend.

They continued to be moved along. Rory noticed some houses had been broken into. Doors and doorframes were busted. Windows were smashed and missing here and there. Russet Road connected with another residential road and they carried on walking. He had never been this way before, though he could see it led through to the centre of the city. Tall buildings sprouted up in that direction, but you probably had to cross a lot of busy roads.

"Look Cam," said Rory quietly. "They're not fighting in the sky any more. The angels and demons. Do you think that means they went back to battle in the mezzanine?"

"No, I think they are just invisible now. But they're still up there."

"You reckon?" Rory made his eyes wide.

The Dream Fighters didn't mind the people talking amongst themselves. That was permitted. Their conversation was diluted by the wide open space above them. As they walked, the noise of the people sounded to Rory like a babbling stream. Water tumbling over rocks and pebbles. The huge volume of people meant they moved very slowly and, fortunately, this accommodated the elderly, the disabled, and the young.

Eventually, the road connected with another couple of roads which led them onto the main arterial thoroughfare, Roasting Vale Lane. In the distance, Rory could see the larger city buildings:

office towers, shops and apartment blocks. But they weren't walking that way. Instead, the channel of people turned right to merge with an overwhelming number of citizens who were shuffling up Roasting Vale. They were flanked by armed Dream Fighter soldiers who stood at the roadside and brandished their weapons menacingly to make sure everyone got the message.

Usually occupied by cars and buses, this four-lane avenue looked completely different. There were people everywhere. Rory closed his eyes a moment. He listened to the chaotic hubbub. A beehive came to mind.

When he opened them again, he was struck by the massive volume of hair all around him. Seeing mostly the backs of people's heads, he realised there really was a very broad spectrum of colours when it came to hair. Although many people had black, brown or fair locks, the ones that stood out were red, blue or pink. And of course, white, like Caleb. It was when he decided to see how many white-haired people he could find that he spied Lake Emerson.

"That's Lake Emerson, Rachel's friend. Over there," he said declaratively to his mum.

"No, sweetie. Lake doesn't have white hair. He's got light blondie-brown hair. Like treacle."

The man in the distance turned around, casting his gaze around. He was located on the left side of the crowd, quite a distance away.

"Oh, sorry honey. My mistake. That is Lake Emerson. You are so right. And look at his hair. So white. I wonder if that means..." Arabella caught Daniels eye and saw that he was also looking over at Lake.

"That's great," he said. "He made it. And, yes, he's met him face to face. Caleb, Serena, over there."

"Yes, I saw him too," Caleb noted.

"Is Rachel with him?" asked Arabella, squinting into the distance.

"I can't see her," said Caleb. "Or Eddie for that matter. Just

Lake. He looks like he's on his own."

Caleb called out to Lake in a loud voice. But it wasn't enough to get his attention. There were too many people in the way, bobbing like buoys in the water.

However, an opportunity arose very soon. Three big men must have made an agreement to rush The Dream Fighters on the left. These guards were the only thing standing between the men and their freedom. The three of them bolted simultaneously to the left. Their assault was swift and unexpected. They each shoulder-barged a different guard, tackling low, knocking them over. Rory felt like he was in the middle of a rugby match.

A good number of people, men and women, broke off from the crowd and followed the men into the side roads of Griffton city centre. They were hotly pursued by other Dream Fighters.

"Quick. This is our chance to move," said Caleb.

"What? Follow them?" asked Arabella, aghast.

"No – I mean catch up with Lake. Come on, grab hands. Push through. Follow me."

"Right you are," Daniel commented. "Kids, ready for this?"

They nodded. Quickly, they slipped past the couple in front, then the group ahead of them, and then half a dozen elderly people. The guards to the left picked themselves up from the ground. But their attention was on the street, not the crowd.

Gunshots rang out. People screamed. More gunshots. Then silence.

"Keep moving forward," said Caleb over his shoulder. "Be brave. Nearly there." They pressed on past even more people, some of whom complained as the six of them broke through.

As she went, Arabella apologised, "Sorry. So sorry. This is an emergency. We must get through with our children. Make way there please. Sorry."

Last summer, Rory's parents had gone to see his dad's favourite rock band at the Griffton Arts Centre. It was a really popular group called "Food Fighters" or something, he couldn't remember exactly. Anyway, his dad said there were people absolutely everywhere. More than the venue should have held. Like when you put too many popcorn kernels in the pan and they all explode and almost overflow.

So, his dad told them he wanted to go down from their seats into the middle of the crowd in front of the stage. He said he wanted their mum to experience what it was like to feel the drums and the bass in her body. Because she'd never been to a gig like that. It sounded crazy fun to Rory and his dad agreed that it was a great concert.

The journey through the crowd felt how he imagined that concert to be. Only without the music. Pushing past people. Trying hard not to step on toes. Being careful not to lose each other. If only he was a bit taller, thought Rory.

Chapter 26

They quickly made it to Lake Emerson. As they embraced him, the Dream Fighters restored order. They menaced the citizens at the edges, making them recoil. In response, the crowd pressed hard against Caleb and the group, like a strong tide lapping at the shore.

"It is so good to see you all," said Lake wistfully.

"Your hair!" shrieked Rory.

"Just like yours," Lake nodded to Caleb. "Yes. I met him. I met the Rescuer. He changed my life. I hear him now, his Dunamis. It's amazing. I mean, I'm a journalist and it's beyond what I can describe. Beyond incredible. It's like I'm completely alive now. Like I wasn't even living before. I get what you guys have been going on about. I get it completely now."

Caleb responded, "That's great. How about Rachel? Eddie? Are they with you? Are they all right?"

"I'm so sorry." Lake looked glum. "We completed our mission. We got to the mountains. The Protector: did you get to see one?" Everyone nodded.

The words tumbled out of Rory: "Ours was on an island in the middle of the ocean. I got to dance on the water and then he came. He was the biggest thing I ever saw. And light came out of him!"

Lake smiled. "How about you?" he asked Daniel.

But Micah answered instead. "It was incredible, just like you

116

said. Ours came out of a massive crater in Africa. I got to activate it with a boy called Ndege, a new friend. He lost his finger, but the Rescuer gave it back. But tell us, how are Rachel and Eddie?"

Lake looked miserable. "Rachel got taken in the mountains. We couldn't stop them. There were two Dream Fighters. Big and fast. We tried but we lost her. And Eddie got hurt. He hurt his ankle. I don't know where she is now."

"How about Eddie?" Caleb asked.

"Eddie couldn't walk. They got him. He didn't make it. The enemy got him."

"Killed?" asked Cameron.

Lake nodded. "I'm so sorry." He sighed deeply. "I had to leave him. He's buried in the snow in Bhutan."

"But he knows the Rescuer, right?" Cameron continued. Lake nodded. "That means we'll definitely see him again. Because if you know the Rescuer, then you never die. You live forever."

"Who Is the Rescuer?" asked a stranger next to them. He was a dark man in his fifties, with greying black hair and thick eyebrows. His brow was furrowed. His shoulders slumped.

"Yeah, who is he?" asked a tall woman in her twenties. Anxiety troubled her face. "What do you mean live forever?" she added.

Cameron turned to his dad for help, realising the conversation had been public. Everyone around had been listening. He mouthed the word "sorry".

An alien tune wove around them. Hovering at a sub-audible level. Rising and falling in pitch and crescendo, if it were to be heard. It caressed the hearts of the people as they eavesdropped on the conversation. Many hearts were weary but open. Others were indifferent. Some were tightly closed.

Nevertheless, a significant number of people were thirsty to drink the words of explanation that came from Daniel. And so he led a lot of people in the throng around them into a relationship with the Rescuer. As they sparked into life and enjoyed the presence of the Dunamis for the very first time, the Dream Fighters looked on, completely unaware.

117

A supernatural peace fell over the group. It radiated outwards as though Caleb, Serena and the Harcourts were a campfire, heating the shivering crowd. They were fire starters in a cold world, the Rescuer's arsonists, starting fires that would set others alight. A blazing forest that no one could extinguish.

Meanwhile, Serena and Caleb had words of encouragement from the Rescuer for individuals. For others the group had personal insights that set them free. Some people were physically healed: a woman with a broken knee; a blind boy who regained his sight. Rory loved every minute of it.

By now, the crowd was shuffling up the road gradually. Aware that something was happening in the mob, the Dream Fighters began to get agitated as they moved people on.

Decrees went out that the crowd was to be quiet as they walked. The soldiers made examples of some people. They beat them mercilessly. Rory became very scared. For the sake of the citizens, Daniel and the rest fell silent. Although they were desperate for people to find freedom, they didn't want them to get injured by the enemy.

After walking in silence for twenty minutes or so, Daniel said to Caleb, "Wherever they're taking us, it isn't going to be good."

"I'm feeling that too. They're up to something but they want us alive. Otherwise they would have killed us in the house."

"Should we be ready to run?"

"Always," grinned Caleb.

It was a long and slow journey up to Griffton Cliff. The path narrowed, making it impossible for the guards to police every section of it. Consequently, the group found the liberty to fall into hushed conversation with those around them. Particularly the ones who had encountered the Rescuer and his Dunamis. They were full of questions which bubbled up continually as they trekked.

The road was steep and winding. The tall trees of North Griffton surrounded them on either side. Fields opened up beyond them. All the while, Griffton Cliff rose resolutely, beckoning them on.

Although their route didn't take them directly past Lytescote Manor, Rory saw its multipronged rooftops in the distance to the west. He couldn't see any obvious signs of damage. Or people, for that matter. He assumed it was crawling with Dream Fighters inside. His heart leapt then sank as they walked past it.

The road wound upwards, amidst complaints of tiredness from all around. Still the Dream Fighters pushed them on. They climbed higher, trudging more slowly up the steep path.

Eventually, they came to Lower Ledge Crossing. The winding road led to the top of the cliff, and a panoramic view over Griffton's devastated rooftops. Whenever he looked back, Rory was shocked all over again. Like he was seeing the broken city for the first time.

The group neared the end of the path which curved gently upwards, taking them to the summit of Griffton Cliff. The wind blew strongly into their faces, north to south. Caleb grabbed hold of Serena's hand. He noticed she was crying quietly. She could feel waves of evil rolling off the top of the cliff.

It wasn't long before they were standing at the summit. The soldiers split people up into groups of thousands. They were made to congregate in particular areas in different fields. Rory quickly realised why everyone was being herded up here. The stone statue of Samyaza towered over their heads several fields away. A heavy blanket of evil lay over them.

It was a marvel they hadn't seen the thing from the road, so tall was the dark angel. It was as big as a castle. The height of four or five trees, Rory calculated. He saw its dark wings which were twice as long as it was high. Rory shivered and looked away, his heart feeling sick to the core.

Chapter 27

Rachel's Diary

Day 4. Seven days. That's all he gave me. Seven days. I only have three left. Three days of life on earth. And today was a long and painful one. Today, they beat me. Really badly. Though it wasn't all bad, believe it or not. I'll tell you about it because I want to write it down. Even though it was so difficult. So bear with me and I'll tell you everything.

In the morning, I found it really hard to hear my new friends, Jia Li, Ndege and Paolo. I listened hard as well. But their voices were quieter. Like the sea in the morning. I used to hear it whispering to me from my bedroom. I like to have my curtains and the window open, you see. And the sea would whisper quietly. I could hear it going about its business. Even though it was way down past the roads and the houses, down beyond the beach. Anyway, I could hear their voices like that. They were talking but I couldn't make out the words. It was kind of frustrating. Like I was missing out on the party.

The guards came in and changed my lightbulb. I didn't see them doing it. I must have been deeply asleep. I wondered if the others also had new lightbulbs. It must have made the enemy very angry, all of our lights breaking at the same time. I bet they wondered what happened. A power surge maybe? Wrong.

It happened quite early, the first beating. But just before the big Dream Fighters came in, Samantha visited me. She tapped me on the arm, waking me up. I looked at her face and she seemed agitated. She glanced at me but looked away quickly.

"I'm sorry," was all she said. Then she left. I quickly worked out why.

Soon after that, the mean ones came in. They forced me to sit on a chair. I thought maybe they were going to feed me. Then one of them said, like he didn't really care either way, "Are you going to follow him?"

I shook my head. Then I looked at him and said, "I follow the Rescuer." After all, I only have three days to live, so why not? He might as well know I'm serious.

He punched me hard in the face. He had a big fist too. It caught the top of my cheek and the side of my eye. It was so painful. I went into shock, more or less straight away I reckon. What happened was just so unexpected. My body went cold and I started shaking.

I don't really remember the next bit of time. It's pretty much a blur to be honest. Like when you stand on a motorway bridge and look down. The cars flash by but you don't really see them. But they fill your head as they whizz past. The beating was like that.

They both took turns jabbing and punching me from the back, front and sides. My arms ached too much to lift them up in defence. Like a boxer numb with exhaustion. I even fell off the chair a couple of times. But they just picked me up, plonked me down and carried on. It was like being in an endless car crash that goes on and on. There was a particularly painful blow to the back of my head that jarred my brain. That one I definitely remember.

Eventually, they left me lying and groaning on the floor. A ragdoll, tossed into the corner by an angry brat. One of my eyes wasn't working. With the other one I could see blood on the floor. My blood. My skin was on fire. My muscles ached and my head throbbed. My left ribs felt broken. Snapped maybe. I was slipping into unconsciousness. The pain was worse than the finger.

As the fog descended over my mind, I felt like I was sliding into a pool of water: Rachel's Pool in the mezzanine. I was right back there. Except I couldn't be. Somebody had broken it down, I remembered. Surely? I saw it with my own eyes when we went back. With Lake and the others. It was in pieces.

But here I was, floating in Rachel's Pool which felt like a massive hot tub, only bottomless. I slipped under the surface. Dunamis waves washed over me. Bathing me. There was no way they could destroy my pool. They could try. Because it wasn't a physical place. It was outside of time and space. Untouchable.

"Rachel's Pool is in your heart," said the Rescuer's voice. It was like when you sip creamy hot chocolate and it slides down your throat, warming everything. Heating you up from the inside. He was still with me. My heart leapt to hear him. It was so exciting. And in that placeless place, outside time, I wept. Life was cruel; Samyaza was cruel but the Rescuer was good. He was kind to me. Even in the presence of my enemies. I finally understood it. The mystery of suffering.

Water caressed. Pain dissolved. Hope returned.

People, circumstances, they inflict pain, but my King is good. I realised my ribs no longer hurt. My eye felt better. It was so strange.

"I love you Rachel Race," said the Rescuer. His rich voice gave the word 'love' so much depth.

"I make all things new," he added. "I will make all things new." I was overjoyed to hear him again. Peace came to me. I drifted into a deep sleep, still floating there in Rachel's Pool. There were no dreams, just rest.

When I woke up, still lying on the floor, I felt no pain. I should have done, but I didn't. I noticed right away that he'd given me my finger back. He really did make all things new. It was the little finger of my left hand. The one the creature had taken. The one Zed sewed onto the Malkin's hand. I've missed it so much. The Rescuer made me whole again.

I cried for a long time after that.

Chapter 28

Rachel's Diary

Later on, Samyaza visited me. I kind of expected it, to be honest. It still unnerved me to be in the same room as him. His head jerked a little too fast. Or he twitched unnaturally. Moving his dark wings suddenly. Grimacing mid sentence. He brought in that familiar stench with him. Rotting meat and sweaty leather. It filled my little cell, right up to the high ceiling. It made the back of my throat hurt.

"We destroyed your home you know," was what he started with. But I was in such a deep place of peace with the Dunamis that I really didn't care. In reality, he might have wrecked the house or he might not. I decided that if I didn't let him get to me, then he couldn't. Besides, I was dead in three days either way. And a pile of bricks is a pile of bricks at the end of the day, whether I lived or died. You know what I mean? They'd already taken my father. There was nothing left for me at home. Nothing.

I noticed Samyaza lock onto my left hand with his eyes. My new finger. He lingered on it. But he didn't choose to say anything.

"Time is passing, Rachel Race. It's amusing to me how quickly time passes for humans," Samyaza observed. "Which means you have just seventy-two hours remaining. Which is nothing really if you think about it. The thing is, everyone bows their knee to me in the end. You might as well do it now. Or I could carry on stripping things away. Piece by piece. And when everything is stripped away and there's nothing left, you will turn to me and follow me."

I didn't say a word through his whole pathetic speech. It felt like the best way to get through it. A bit like when a teacher gives you a lecture. The thought did pass through my mind that I could take the knife and plunge it into his back as he left. But by the way he moved, I guessed he would retaliate with supernatural force. I would end up dead and it would be suicide. A bit like suicide by cop, when you attack an armed officer. Pointless really. I didn't want to play that game. I'm not going out like that.

"Perhaps you're ready for me to send my guards back in? They could continue the conversation they began this morning. Although it doesn't look like they did a very thorough job. Did they go soft on you little girl? Because of your big, sad eyes? Is that right, Rachel Race?"

I still had thick patches of dried blood on my body. I couldn't be bothered to wash it off. I could also see bruises on my arms and sides, though there was no pain or swelling beneath.

Suddenly, the Dunamis rose up inside me and I laughed hard in Samyaza's face. It was the phrase "big, sad eyes" that triggered me. I had a vivid picture of myself looking like a big cartoon puppy. My laughter was explosive, uncontrollable. Offensive.

Samyaza stood and stared. It was like he didn't know what to do. Like nobody ever laughed at him. I'd smacked him right in the face with a golf club. That dumb fallen angel with a God complex.

He turned and left quickly through the open door. I grinned as one of the guards pulled it closed, making it clank shut. Still smiling, I moved to the back of my cell and collapsed on the bed.

°°°°°*12345*°°°°°

Samantha came to check on me. She crept in quietly. When she saw me she took in a sharp intake of breath. "Oh, Rachel. What have they done to you?"

124

"Says the jailer. I've had better days," I snapped. It felt like one of my old conversations with Lara.

"Are you okay?"

"Yeah, I'm okay. It doesn't hurt any more. It looks worse than it feels."

"Let me clean you up?" She pulled a cloth from within her uniform. Next, she ran it under the tap and wiped my arms gently.

"What's the point? They'll only do it again. And in three days I'll be dead."

"I am not happy about what's going on here."

"So what? Me neither."

Samantha pulled off her big Dream Fighter's cap. It was like the first time I met her. All that time ago. Three days ago. Her long blonde hair tumbled out. I wondered how she managed to hide so much of it in there. It was a bit like a magic trick. Pulling silk handkerchiefs out of your sleeve or something.

She handed me a banana and I ate it ravenously without thanking her. Then she found a chocolate bar. These things were literally life savers. I helped myself to a glass of water from my sink.

"Listen, I know what they're doing is wrong," she said.

"That makes two of us."

"It's wrong and I'm going to help you," she added quietly.

"Is this a trick?"

She looked down, "No Rachel. This isn't a trick. You need to listen out around three in the morning."

"I don't have a way to tell the time."

"Sorry, of course you don't."

"What time is it now?"

She looked at her watch. "It's eight o'clock now." Then she unclipped her watch and handed it to me.

"You sure?"

She nodded hard. "It's okay. I still have my phone to tell the time. So anyway, keep your ears open. They change the guards at three and leave the rooms unattended for a while. Half an hour or so. They all go to the room to be with him. The master. Do their funny rituals. Blood sacrifices, I think." She shivered. "I don't get included. Anyway, they don't expect any trouble at that time. So, in the night, I'm going to come and open your door."

"Are you sure? What if they catch you?"

"I'm small and fast. I'll be back in my room before they know it. But if I do this, you'll be on your own."

"Okay," I said.

She spoke quickly. "Once out of your room, make a right. That corridor meets another one. Turn right again. Go down the corridor until you get to the steps that lead to the shower room. They will be on the right of you. Go up those stairs until you get to the showers near the top. The corridor keeps on going past them. But there is a small door beyond the shower room. It leads to a flight of stairs that goes up. I don't think anyone uses them at night."

"Why are you helping me?"

"Just be careful. And get far away from here."

"What about the others? There are other prisoners in this place."

"I know. But I can't help everyone. Just you. Maybe you can get out and get help."

"Maybe."

"Right, I have to go. I really hope I never see you again, Rachel. And remember: make a right, down the corridor, right up the stairs, right past the showers and left through the door."

"I got it the first time."

"It's been nice knowing you Rachel Race."

"You too Samantha…"

"Grace. My name's Samantha Grace."

I giggled and Samantha looked offended. I explained, "It's funny. Our names rhyme. Race and Grace."

"Yeah, funny." Samantha nodded, but she looked serious. "Okay, bye."

She left almost as quickly as Samyaza had, leaving me staring at the door.

Of course I found it almost impossible to sleep. I ended up writing all this. The light that never goes out helps me see the paper.

Lying on my bed, I reached out to my friends. I didn't really want to tell them about the escape plan in case they got tortured. It is unlikely, but I really didn't want anything to get in the way.

It went through my mind that it is, in reality, a terrible plan. Full of things that could go wrong. An early exchange of guards. A shorter meeting with the master. Dream Fighters hanging out on the steps. Locked doors. Ending up in a maze of corridors. So many potential problems.

Then Jia Li's cheery voice popped into my mind, "Today was a good day. They left me alone but gave me lots of food. How about you, Rachel?"

"Today they beat me."

"Oh no! Are you hurt?"

"No. I mean I was. I think they cracked my ribs. And they busted up my eye. And my head. But the Rescuer came to me. He fixed me up good. I even got my finger back like Ndege."

"That's amazing!" said Ndege.

"Oh, hi Ndege. I didn't know you were there," I said.

He replied, "I had a boring day today. Perhaps they'll beat me tomorrow. And I miss my father."

"Oh, my invisible friends. How I love you. Let's hope we can escape soon," I said.

"Yes, let's hope," said Paolo, who was also there in my head.

Then Jia Li said, "Would anyone like to hear some more Du Fu?"

"Sure. Why not," I said. And off she went.

"This one is a short poem called Overflowing. He wrote it in the year seven sixty-six. He talks about the night. Night is divided into five watches and the third watch is midnight. Are you all ready?"

"Yes, tell us," I encouraged her.

When she spoke, her words unfolded in my head like a flower.

"The moon's reflected on the river a few feet away. A lantern shines in the night near the third watch. On the sand, egrets sleep, peacefully curled together. Behind the boat I hear the splash of jumping fish."

Chapter 29

Rachel's Diary

Samantha Grace's watch is small and silver. I hid it under my pillow and checked on it every so often. It was a precious prize. Its face told me the time was ten past eight when Samantha left. And when Jia Li finished her poem, it was a quarter to nine. Being able to tell the time gave me a new confidence. Incredibly, the powers that be decided to give me some dinner. This was unexpected. It was hot too.

The tray arrived at nine twenty-one. Some sort of heated-up meat pie with a pastry crust and peas from a can. It all tasted fab to me. There was a can of fizzy drink as well and a chocolate muffin in a plastic wrapper. If I thought they had a heart, then this would be them saying sorry for torturing me. But of course they didn't. So they weren't. This was probably just food to keep me alive until the next beating. Or else they weren't going to feed me for the rest of my time in captivity. At midnight, I will only have two days left to live.

The only problem with having a watch is time passes painfully slowly. I tried to take my time eating the meal. But I only managed to stretch it to eleven minutes because I was hungry.

They came and took the tray away at five minutes to ten. Both times they visited, nobody asked me the question. I think they knew what the answer would be. They closed the door and left me alone again.

On a whim, I decided to ask my invisible friends a question. "Jia Li. Are you there?"

"Yes, Rachel."

"Jia Li. Do you know whereabouts we are?"

"I think we are underground."

"Me too. Do you know where your cell is?"

"No. I might be in the middle of a long corridor. I don't know for sure."

"Paolo. You?"

"I am definitely in an end room."

"How do you know?"

"It's quiet here. And I peeked through the blindfold once."

"That's great."

"Ndege, any idea where you are? Have you seen a long corridor with lots of doors and lights in the ceiling?"

"No. I don't know where I am."

"I think I hear you sometimes," said Jia Li.

"What do you mean?" asked Ndege.

"You sing a song, right? One where you clap three times."

"Yes, how do you know?"

"Sometimes I hear you. Sing it now, Ndege."

"Okay. I will sing it for you. Only I will sing in Swahili. You tell me if you hear me clapping. It goes like this: Moja, mbili, tatu, nne, tano, nimepata samaki, mkubwa mno. Nawe mwenye nguvu, kwanini ukamuwachia? Kaniuma kidole. Nalia eee, eee."

"Yes, I can hear you clapping three times. It isn't very loud. I think you are next to me. Your cell is next to me, I mean," Jia Li said.

"So, we are neighbours."

"Yes we are."

I lay back on the bed and asked, "So Ndege, what does your song mean? Why the three claps?"

"It is a song we used to sing when I was small. My mother taught me. It cheers me up. It goes like this: One, two, three, four, five, I got a big fish, very big. And you who has strength, why did you let it go? It bit my finger. I cry, "eee, eee!"."

"No offence, but that is, like, the creepiest song. Don't you think? It reminds me of someone I met in the mezzanine. He was a creepy beast. Anyway, we have a nursery rhyme just like it in English but I'm not going to sing it," I informed him.

So anyway, I wrote all this up. Then I closed my eyes. Meanwhile, my friends chatted quietly to one another. I must've fallen asleep after that.

°°°°°12345°°°°°

Rachel's Diary

Day 5. It was two forty five in the morning when I woke up. I panicked. I couldn't find the watch. I scratched around desperately under the pillow. Then I spotted it. It was on the floor. When I saw the time, I quickly got up and went to the door. It was still shut and locked. I paced around to wake myself up. If Samantha was able to get away, the door would be open soon. Adrenalin started to rush through my body.

I stood waiting in my tracksuit bottoms, hooded top and thick socks. Listening. It was two minutes to three. I was desperate to get out. My room felt suffocating.

True to her word, Samantha opened the metal door at three in the morning.

"Ready?" she hissed. "The coast is clear."

"Yeah," I whispered back.

I heard her treading lightly away. I breathed in through my nose and pushed open the door. Outside, I saw a bright corridor with yellow lights high up on the ceiling, spaced regularly. The passageway ran left to right.

"Okay, Rachel. You've got thirty minutes. You can do this," I told myself. "Do a right out of the room. Corridor. Then right again. Corridor. Right up the stairs. Go past the showers. Open the door on the left. And climb, climb, climb for freedom. Easy peasy."

131

It was cool outside my room. Even with my thick socks and hoodie on. I took a deep breath and went along the passage. It was hard and cold under my feet. I spied the right turn ahead. All of a sudden, the Dunamis leapt inside me. It was like the time I met Jia Li in the corridor. It's hard to explain. It's a bit like when one magnet rushes towards another.

"Rachel?" Ji Lia was in my head.

"You awake?"

"Rachel, you are outside my room."

I stopped in my tracks and turned to look at the door to my left. "How do you know?" But even as I asked the question, the Dunamis confirmed it.

I took the handle in both hands and pulled it up and then down. Nothing. It wouldn't budge.

"I can't get it open," I told her in my mind. I heard a clicking from within, as she tried to yank it.

Chapter 30

Rachel's Diary

"I have an idea," I said. "Do you remember our lightbulbs? We smashed them through the power of the Dunamis?"

"Yes. You focus on the door handle. I will do the same."

In seconds, the door was open and I was embracing my new friend, a small and muscular Chinese girl. We were dressed identically. She had big round eyes and long, black hair. Just as I'd imagined. I instantly liked her a lot.

"Ndege. He is next to me. Let's get him."

"Which room?"

She indicated the room to the left. We both concentrated on the door handle, felt power go through us and watched it click open.

"Amazing," she said.

We quickly pulled open the door. A boy was asleep on the bed.

"Ndege, wake up," I whispered harshly. It took a while for him to come round. When he did, he was confused. The boy didn't look particularly African to me. More South American.

"Quién eres tú?" he said, rubbing his eyes.

"Ndege, it's Rachel and Jia Li."

"I am José," he declared proudly. As he spoke, I felt the Dunamis well up inside me with love for this young man. Power seemed to glue the three of us together. I saw he was missing a finger.

"You're the fifth," I gasped. "Do you know the Rescuer?"

"He is my enemy," spat José. "He is no good." Then he looked sad. "But the Dream Fighters are no better. They tricked me. I don't trust anyone."

"Well, that's okay. The Rescuer loves you anyway," I told him. "And he chose you. Come on, you're escaping with us today."

José didn't argue. We all went outside into the corridor. In no time, we got the metal door open on the other side of Jia Li's cell. Ndege, and it was Ndege this time, rushed out and hugged us all. Like me, he had all his fingers now. He was a head shorter than me, dark-brown and skinny. I liked his face straight away. It was so happy.

"It is a pleasure to meet you, Rachel. Jia Li. And who is this?" Ndege had a lovely voice. Full of life.

"I am José," he said grumpily, and then smiled unexpectedly. He wasn't all bad. Actually, he was quite good-looking, with shaggy dark hair and cocoa-coloured skin. He spoke with a gorgeous accent.

"Good to meet you, José," said Ndege confidently. "I am Ndege from Tanzania."

"Hey, you speak Spanish too?"

"No," said Ndege, shaking his head. "Not me. Just Swahili and English."

"Well, I hear you in Spanish. I hear you all in Spanish."

"The Dunamis. He translates for us," Jia Li said. José looked confused, but shrugged his shoulders and smiled.

A strange feeling of joy fell on us. My heart was fluttering. It was a good thing that was happening. I checked my watch. It was already three fifteen. Where had the time gone? Well, I knew where it had gone. We were hanging around and chatting when we should really be running.

"We need to find Paolo," said Ndege. "No one gets left behind."

"Agreed. He said he was at the end of a corridor. How do we find him?"

"It's this way," Ndege said, pointing back the way I'd come.

"Are you sure?"

"He's this way. The Dunamis told me." Ndege set off at a pace back down the corridor. He was like a little bird, hopping along. We had no choice but to follow.

Sure enough, there was one room at the end of the corridor. Jia Li, Ndege and I stared at the door and asked the Dunamis to open it. Meanwhile, the new guy, José, stood there and smirked. He stopped grinning when the door broke open though, and just stared.

A young man, slightly taller than the four of us, walked slowly out, rubbing his eyes with one hand. He had a pair of glasses in the other.

"The Rescuer told me you would come," he said quietly. "I am Paolo. Good to meet you all." He seemed very relaxed.

I gave him a quick hug which made him blush. Nice to have that sort of power, I thought. Then, checking my watch, I said, "Time's getting on. We'd better run. The guards are back in a few minutes."

José looked horrified.

I led them back along the corridor past my room, then beyond José, Ndege and Jia Li's prison cells.

As Samantha had reminded me, this corridor met another long one. We turned right and kept going. Still no one in sight. Very soon, we got to the right turn that led to the next level. Stone steps. I stopped and listened. Silence upstairs. I took the lead.

"Follow me." Up we went, past the shower room and a few steps down a long, straight corridor. The door was exactly where Samantha had said, beyond the shower room and to the left. I pulled it open.

Inside was a stairwell that ran up and down. It wound around and around to the right. My guess was that we were in the bowels of Lytescote Manor, down in some sort of underground complex. This stairway was our route to freedom. It would lead us up to the main part of the house. There, we'd do our best to escape the enemy. Climb out of a window. Find that fireplace tunnel. Or run down the driveway, past that funny looking mini tower, and out of the gates.

Checking my watch quickly, I saw it was already three thirty-five. We had gone beyond the time, but the guards hadn't returned. "We're going up," I told my friends. And so, we started to climb the stairs. The order we went up in was: me, Jia Li, Ndege, Paolo and then José.

Just as José went through the door, I heard him yelp and call out, "Guards!"

We began to jump up two or three steps at a time.

"Everyone okay?" I shouted. Several of them said yes, but I heard José yell, "Quick. They're coming!"

They chased us up those stairs, me and Jia Li taking the lead, climbing almost next to each other. The boys followed close behind. Boy, I felt scared, I can tell you. We could hear the sound of the Dream Fighters: heavy steps on the stairs below.

"We have to do something, Jia Li." We went past another door. I thought about opening one of them and taking our chances on a different floor. Samantha said the stairs go up. But she didn't say when to stop climbing!

"We push them back. With the power. We press them back," Jia Li commanded.

I broadcasted the words: "Everyone, in your minds, ask the Dunamis to push them back!" And so we did.

Then it happened. We heard the sound of tumbling and slumping, falling and collapsing. We carried on going. We'd stopped the enemy. We were free for now. Interestingly, instead of making us go more slowly, we actually sped up. I guess we're all fit.

The stairwell ended unexpectedly. We got to a place where it just didn't go up any further. There was a final door that looked just like the other ones. White, featureless. We all stood on that final landing. A rectangle that just about fit the five of us.

I said, "This is it. Whatever's on the other side, we face it together. And we face it with the power of the Dunamis. Right José? You've seen what the Rescuer and his Dunamis can do. Are you with us?"

He nodded. "Okay then, let's go."

I turned the handle and pushed the heavy door. It opened onto a massive stony rooftop. There was nowhere to go beyond the edges. Just a long, long drop. As I stepped out, I saw the swirling violet and magenta sky of the mezzanine. Black mountain peaks surrounded us. The sky was full of black demons, flying around like evil ravens. On the steps behind us, I could hear the Dream Fighters.

"What is this wicked place?" said Ndege.

I screamed long and hard in response.

Chapter 31

"This is not over," roared Ndege, staring at the sky. I think he took all of us by surprise. Such a loud noise coming from someone his size.

"Quick, let's do that thing we did on the stairs," he added. "Everybody! Push those guards back again. Ask the Dunamis. Come on!"

I felt the Dunamis swell my heart. "Yeah, let's do this," I agreed. I found myself giggling, but also full of confidence that this would work. After all, it did last time. Those Dream Fighters were flesh and blood like us. And we had the advantage of being friends of the King.

I closed my eyes. I assume the others did the same but maybe they didn't. I guess we all focused anyway. Several sets of footsteps landed heavily at the top of the stairs. I opened my eyes and saw them. They were big men. Armed and angry-looking. I remember one of them had a cut on his cheek that looked like it was a recent thing.

Sure enough, the Dream Fighters stopped still and scowled. Held back by an invisible hand. They knew something wasn't right. Then they groaned and tumbled backwards down the stairs. It was almost comical. Like a cartoon or a Marx Brothers film. Like somebody had thrown a bowling ball at them. Nine pins scattering. They disappeared out of sight.

"How many of them do you think there are?" José asked.

"I don't know. Four or five maybe. Hard to tell. Maybe more behind. But I think we're better off inside than outside, with those things up there," replied Ndege.

So we decided to go back to the stairwell and shut the roof door. José leaned against it just in case. Our plan was we would go down to a lower floor and stay inside the building. Stay away from the demons. If we found any more Dream Fighters, we knew what to do. We all agreed we would prefer to take our chances with the guards than tangle with the monsters out there. We'd gone past lots of doors on the stairs, so surely one of them would give us an exit?

Suddenly, we didn't have a choice. The door was ripped off its hinges with supernatural force. José jumped and clung onto us. Standing outside was one of those big winged creatures. Like the ones I met in the mezzanine last time. I'd survived their attack back then because the angels protected me. But this time, there weren't any rescuers. Just a purple sky full of killing machines. We were on our own.

We heard a commotion below. The Dream Fighters were up on their feet again. They were coming back up. It was like something out of the Terminator. Evil robots that don't know when to stop. Or are unable to stop.

"Let's do that thing again," yelled José. His eyes were wild. "Maybe we can do it both ways? Blast them both backwards!"

I liked this idea a lot. I felt my body swell with the power of the Dunamis. "Okay," I said.

"Everyone ready?" called José, taking charge.

"Dunamis, we desperately need your help," I whispered, and closed my eyes.

When I opened them again, the demon in front had gone and the footsteps had stopped. It had worked! Jia Li yelped with delight, grinning like a fool. Then she ran out of the open doorway and shot onto the roof.

"Jia Li, no!" I cried out. "We need to go back down. Find

another door." But it was too late. She was sprinting along the roof, trying to break for freedom. Nothing could stop her. She was like a crazy person. I looked up to see if anything was coming her way. Nope, all good for now. They were circling high above and the roof was clear.

Paolo spotted something in the distance. A small building that looked like it could give us some protection. Jia Li was already running for it. It looked like a shack or a lookout tower with rounded edges instead of a neat roof, like it was moulded by hand.

"Come on. Let's stick together," I said. "If we have to do that blast thing again, it works better when we are all together."

So we made the decision to run: to follow Jia Li along the grey roof. Ndege and I went first. The other two were close behind. Fortunately, apart from that one big creature at the door, the others stayed in the air for now.

The purple sky made everything look really weird. My friends' faces looked particularly strange, beetroot-coloured and unwell. The place smelt like bad eggs. I guess the huge number of leathery monsters in the sky made the whole place reek. It was like when they lay manure in the fields around Griffton. Because of it, the bit around Griffton Cliff stinks like warm Marmite.

We got to the safe place quickly. It was a grey lookout tower made of clay, with two entrances but no doors. It wasn't very big inside and had windowless openings with views of the mountains. But it did have a ceiling. That gave us some protection from the monsters above, if they decided to attack. We huddled together.

"What do we do?" asked José. "I don't like the look of these things. I have seen some bad things in my time. But these are the worst."

"I agree," said Ndege. "I don't like their teeth or their claws." He shivered.

"We need to find a way to get off the roof," Jia Li said. "There has to be a way to get down to the bottom and away from here."

"It looks like we're very high up," said Paolo.

I glanced around the rooftop and saw a couple of other grey bunkers like this one. Not much could be seen beyond them. It wasn't clear how big the roof was either.

"Remember, if one of those black things comes down here, we blast it," said Ndege.

"I don't think we should stay here," Paolo chipped in. He turned away to look out of the window. Black winged creatures flew high up in the air, with a line of dark mountains behind them. The coast was clear for now.

Chapter 32

I wondered which part of the mezzanine we were in. The land itself could be as big as the earth or it might be a hundred times bigger. I've probably only seen a fraction of it in reality. A valley or two, Zed's house, some fields, a forest, Rachel's Pool, the caves and that river. Nothing much really. It might link to other worlds as well as the Earth. Who knows?

Suddenly, talons appeared at the window and swiped at Paolo. I saw a long arm and a thick black wing, attached to a leathery body. The demon outside stared through two tiny black eyes. It had no human emotions I could read. Horrible.

"It's got my sleeve!" Paolo cried. "Knock it back!" The demon's strong arm pulled Paolo violently towards the window. It slammed his side into the wall, bumping his face. His glasses flew off and hit the floor.

I cried out to the Dunamis for help. He came through for me. The next thing, I saw the creature flying backwards. Thrown to the edge of the building. It didn't manage to take Paolo with it, which was a relief. The monster disappeared over the edge. We waited to see it reappear, but it had gone.

"Are you okay, Paolo?" I checked. He rubbed his head and nodded, reaching for his glasses. His face looked grazed.

"We can't stay here," said Jia Li. I agreed.

She left through the second door, Ndege following close

behind. This time he outran her to the next lookout post. It looked exactly the same as the other one, grey with a roof that had rounded edges. It didn't give us any better protection either.

This time, we all kept our eyes on the creatures up in space. They looked agitated. They were moving faster and in formation now. Big loops and figures of eight. Something was keeping them at bay up there. It was somehow stopping them from attacking us. I'm sure they would easily pick us off if they could. We were like worms in the grass, wriggling helplessly and trying to hide from the birds.

"The next one isn't very far. It looks like it's bigger and has a few rooms. What do you think?" I said.

But the others were staring into the distance.

"What is it?"

"Look. Over there," said José. "There are some white ones."

Sure enough, a long line of white winged creatures had appeared far away. Tinged with other colours – blues, greens and yellows. They stayed around the edge, flying really fast.

"Warrior Angels!" I cried. "They're here!"

"They're not close enough," Jia Li said, and sprinted out onto the roof. She skipped like a dancer, small and fast. We all watched her go.

"Man, she's going to get herself killed," Paolo complained.

Just before she got to the next building, a black creature swooped down with lightning speed. We all saw it happening. I'm sure we all called on the Dunamis at the same time, willing it to stop the demon from attacking. I know I did.

Jia Li ran into the building just as the monster got near her. There were a few tense seconds as it approached the doorway. The next bit happened really fast.

Jia Li appeared with a knife in her left hand. It was like the one I had in my cell. The one Samyaza said I could take my life with. He must have told the others the same thing. Hers was jagged and nasty looking, with a cherry-red handle.

She slashed at the demon a couple of times. She looked like a

143

martial arts expert - it wasn't just the fact she was Chinese. The girl really had game. The first swipes went through the air but one of them made contact. She drew it across the monster's body, making it move back. It was very cool to watch.

Next I saw her stab the knife into its body, all the way. She pressed it in with her full force, putting her body behind her attack. I was so proud of her. But the beast swiped back with its claws, like an angry lion. Jia Li caught the talons across her shoulder. But it looked like her knife was slowing the monster down. Now I come to think of it, it was epic and scary all at the same time.

"Everyone. Push it back now," I said to the others from our place of safety. We called on the Dunamis and saw the demon fly backwards quickly. It was like a rope was dragging it over to the side. We watched it tumble over the edge, just like the other one. This one didn't come back either. I imagined it crashing to the ground below. Smashing its body against the rocks.

We ran over to our friend. Jia Li was okay, but bleeding. She stood panting, rooted to the spot. We carried her backwards into the building, moving her away from the door and windows. Ndege stood guard in the doorway, keeping his eyes fixed on the sky.

Jia Li had three long gashes in her shoulder and winced with the pain. I laid my hand on her arm and asked the Rescuer to help. Seconds later, I saw her face relax as the pain left. We felt that strange glowing feeling that comes when we are together in the same place, the five of us. Like we are one person.

"You feel that?" I asked the others. They nodded. We felt the peace and power of the Dunamis run through us like we were electricity cables. There were a few more Warrior Angels in the sky now. They had broken into a large patch of the darkness and were battling hard up there. But they were still heavily outnumbered. I wondered if Mattatron was up there.

José found a door in the corner. It was camouflaged at first which was why we didn't see it. He opened it carefully and said,

"What do you think is in here?"

Before anyone could do anything, he pulled it open the rest of the way. We turned and looked in, seeing a darkened stairwell that went down into the building.

"Good find," said Paolo. "I would love to get off this roof."

"What do you reckon? Should we go in?" I asked Jia Li. But of course I knew the answer.

Chapter 33

Rachel's Diary

Jia Li bravely led us forwards, pushing José aside. Paolo pulled the door closed at the top, shutting out the monsters and the mezzanine night. We wondered if the demons were allowed in the building. Maybe they had to stay outside because they were too wild. They'd probably just wreck the place and the Dream Fighters would have to tidy up. Best keep them outside like the animals they were. That's what I reckoned anyway.

We went down the steps slowly, listening hard. There was just enough light to see. The stairwell was very like the other one. We went past the first landing, all of us deciding it was too near the roof to exit there. It would be a shame to go out too early and get eaten. So we carried on going down. I counted ten more doors, which I calculated would maybe take us to a level above ours.

I suggested, "Why don't we get out here? If we meet any guards, we get ready to floor them."

Jia Li nodded and tried the door. It was locked. The boys were behind us, up the steps. They kept asking what was going on.

"Quiet boys. It's time for our cell door special," I said. "We have a door here but it's locked. Everyone link up and ask the Dunamis to open it. Should be easy, right?"

In no time at all the door was open. We pushed it and went through. Instead of a maze of corridors, we found ourselves in a big room with terracotta walls and a grey stone floor. Nice colours together. Yellow lights in the ceiling lit the room. They were the same ones they used in the corridors and prison cells. The ones we shattered. Must have been a mezzanine job lot. From a demonic superstore that did a special deal on lightbulbs for scary monsters.

There were open doorways in three of the walls. "What do you reckon?" I asked.

"I can't hear the Dunamis about any particular direction," said Ndege. "We could try that one over there. Or split up and try different doors. See what happens?"

"That never works in the movies. Everyone always gets picked off one by one," I said. I looked at the three doorways across the room. "I think we should go for one and stick together. One thing we know for sure is we're stronger together." Everyone seemed to agree.

We decided to move to the furthest point and listen at the doorway. Everything was quiet.

The next room was even bigger. More yellow lights. This time, there were exits in all of the walls. It reminded me of the caves where I'd found Micah after he'd been tricked by Zed and tied up. Those caves went on and on. Big ones. Small ones. Long ones. Low ones. The mezzanine forest was like that as well. Loads of trees and hedges that send you round in circles or end up in dead ends. Enough to drive you nuts.

"Any ideas?" I asked. José shrugged. Paolo looked thoughtful. Ndege and Jia Li were keen to go wherever. They even got ready to race through two different doors but I stopped them.

"We should stick together," I reminded them.

We walked the length of the room and through the door at the end, keeping together. The next room was bigger still with even more doors. It felt like one of the tricks of the mezzanine. Shifting ground. Rocks that hang in the air. Rivers that end in a rocky wall and you have to dive under to get past them. We huddled together in the middle, feeling like it was the safest place.

It was completely unexpected when loads of Dream Fighters

poured in through the doorways. They arrived so fast, we didn't have time to push them back. It was like water seeping through the ceiling and flooding a room. Drowning you. There were more than I could count.

First, they knocked out José with the butt of a sword. It was horrible. I think they cut his head open. Then Ndege and Jia Li got attacked at the same time. I cried out to the Rescuer for help but saw them taking Paolo down. There was nothing I could do.

Just as they came for me, I saw Samyaza appear through the doorway. I felt the horrible feeling you get when he's in the room. Like a black depression. Like the sort of headache that makes you numb. So you can't think. He looked like a huge black spider. The ones that scuttle and jump. He stared at me with those dead eyes. But I think they had a sparkle of hatred in them this time.

"Rachel Race," he said in a low voice, like he was taking a register or something. After that, I thought I heard something like, "Prepare the Valenstriucciae. We need five this time." Then everything went black.

Chapter 34

Rachel's Diary

I found myself back in the cell, stewing and writing furiously. Writing everything down from our night-time escape. Well, our attempted escape. At least they left me my pen and paper. Except my pen is starting to run out and the ink doesn't always flow. That's why my writing is getting a bit thin in places.

Anyway, I checked in with Jia Li, Paolo, Ndege and José. It was six in the morning, day five. I know because I still have Samantha's watch. Fortunately, my friends were all right and no one appeared to have been badly hurt in the ambush. José had a sore head. Jia Li's shoulders hurt where they'd grabbed her, and there were red scoring marks from the talons. If anything, it made them even more determined to get out of their cells again.

I quickly found out they were plotting another escape, believe it or not. But I wasn't so sure about it myself. The problem was the odds were stacked against us. I reminded them we are surrounded by Dream Fighters, Angel Hunters, not to mention Samyaza himself. And he's fast. Plus, we are hidden somewhere in the depths of the mezzanine, not Lytescote Manor, far away from our friends and family. There was no one around who could help us get out. Although we could break open the doors at any time, and probably knock out a guard or two, that would only get us so far. The Angel Hunters are far too quick and Samyaza is even faster. And when they hit us, it really hurts.

Jia Li was fuming. She wanted to find Samyaza and do a joint attack on him: one that removed his head from his shoulders. Ndege was also keen to try out our new powers, though he didn't have a strategy in mind. His preference was to run as fast as possible and even see if we could fly.

But Paolo said, "We need to trust the Rescuer. He knows exactly what is happening. Although he has the power to stop it, maybe it isn't in his plan or timing."

"Well it should be," said José. "If he really knows what he's doing and he's got the power."

Paolo continued, "He has. But it means we have to be patient."

"But I only have a couple of days to live," I complained.

"That's what the enemy says. It doesn't mean it's definitely the case."

"What do you mean?"

Paolo explained, "Remember, it looked like we were trapped in our cells. But we made it to the roof, didn't we? If he wants us rescued, he'll do it. Otherwise, our mission is something else."

"Well, I just wish he'd rescue us soon."

They went a bit quiet after that. Basically, I'm writing this in what must be the afternoon because I caught up on my sleep earlier. My room is as bright as ever, so it could be night or day. Not that you can really tell in the mezzanine. It's got a different clock to the one on earth. The guards are leaving me alone and they haven't given me any food. Strangely though, I don't feel hungry anymore. Now I know we are in the mezzanine.

Being here means you don't really get hungry or tired except in your mind. So if you block it out, you could probably stay awake forever and not be hungry, because something strange happens to your body. Of course you can still feel physical pain. And things like gravity still work because you don't just float off into the purple sky. But when it comes to things like food and sleep, they don't really matter in the same way. Anyway, a brain-box like Paolo probably understands it better than me. I was never that good at school.

Sometime in the afternoon, I got a visit from a guard. He was a big man, like a wrestler.

"Don't try anything, or you'll meet my gun," he growled. "My friends are waiting outside the door just in case. We can make life very hard for you. Just give us an excuse."

I stared at him and kept my mouth shut. We must have got them really scared for them to be this heavy. After all, I'm a little girl; he's a big man. What threat am I?

I noticed he had a cap in his hand. Samantha's cap. He threw it at me and sneered. "We hate traitors."

A cold dread came over me and I think my face betrayed me, because he said, "Yeah, that's what I thought. Like I say, we hate traitors."

"Don't hurt her. It was my fault," I begged.

"Too late for that. We took her to the roof. Our friends up there did the rest. You gave us the idea really."

He laughed as he walked out. Me? I screamed and threw Samantha's cap at him but he was gone. It bounced off the back of the door as it slammed shut, then flopped pathetically on the floor.

I'm so sorry Samantha. I couldn't save you.

°°°°°12345°°°°°

Rachel's Diary

Day 6. It's hard to write now. This morning they put it on my head. The monster. I hate it. It was late. They came in and I saw it behind them. Big and see-through. Like a jellyfish. They held my arms down. Two guards lifted it up. I can't get it off me. I've tried. It's heavy, like a big rubber sack. Like a big jelly. The boys told me about this thing. It's called a Valenstriuccia. Caleb told them. He had one on him. They don't kill you straightaway. They do something worse. Rescuer, help me.

I can still write a bit. Slowly. I think the monster's doing something to my head. My mind. Putting thoughts in. False memories. Can't think. So tired. Can't think straight anymore. Feel drunk. Drugged. Feel sad. Really sad. I see my dad's face. In my head. He stares at me. Like I'm to blame. Like it's my fault. It's too much. I want it to end. All of it. No more writing. Need to close my eyes.

°°°°°12345°°°°°

151

Random fires raged through the city of Griffton. They ravaged both award-winning architecture and functional warehouses alike, darkening the sky with smoke. The stench stretched from the cliff down to the beach.

All the while, Warrior Angels battled continually against Angel Hunters, bent on destruction. Swords, wings and fists swung through the air. They either found their target or smashed into something else. And as they fought, windows vomited their glass. Buildings spewed chunks of masonry. Bricks flew violently, pitting the ground as they landed. Chaos reigned.

The individual Nephilim who was assigned to Griffton howled and heaved an oak up from its roots. He dragged it through a line of cars, its solid branches crunching through their frames. Car alarms wailed. The creature abandoned his tree, leaving it impaled through a windscreen. Something more violent down the road captured his fancy, so off he went.

The Dream Fighters rounded up the majority of the citizens. The ones who were left sprinted into the open, giving up their positions. But they were clawed to death by an Angel Hunter. Or else they got herded towards the main road by the Dream Fighters. And these Sapana guards were driven by demons of their own. Terrified, the citizens let themselves be led slowly up to Griffton Cliff and the malevolent statue that awaited them.

The Dream Fighters' commands were that everyone had to go up to the statue. If they didn't go, they got butchered on the spot. A prospect that filled the people with dread whilst thrilling their captors. Everyone had to bow to Samyaza and there were to be no exceptions. They were the kind of orders Dream Fighters lived for: simple, direct and brutal. Straight from their master, Samyaza.

Besides, everyone bows to him in the end, they reasoned. He was the king of the world, and the king deserves honour and praise. Anything less than that was unacceptable.

Chapter 35

There are some things in life that are just impossible to comprehend, thought Iona. The world tried to cram itself into her huge eyes as she took in the scene. The broad spectrum of colours. The constant movement, like ocean waves. People everywhere of all shapes, sizes and shades. It was like a gig or a music festival, she thought. Only the people weren't happy and there was no music. Unusually for her, she was not in the mood to people-watch today, despite it being one of her best hobbies. In fact, the sheer volume of bodies around her made her feel nauseous.

Then there were the guards. These terrible armoured beasts of people. Angry faces. Leather uniforms. Weapons. They herded the people of Griffton like cattle. Grunting, shouting. Some used the butt of a rifle or a stick to move people on. Others actually used their swords. It was inhuman.

Meanwhile, she could see dark clouds rising up from the valley. Plumes of purple-grey smoke. They were burning the city she loved. Destroying famous buildings. Peoples' homes. It was too much.

She clung tightly to Ben's arm. There was no point hiding her affection for him anymore and he certainly wasn't complaining. He put his hand over hers. She enjoyed his closeness. The strength of his body.

Her friends, Matt, Grace and Sophia, stood near them, secret friends of the Rescuer, banding together. If the guards knew, they would kill them instantly. Apart from Ben and her friends, she didn't know anyone else. The people in the crowd could be locals or tourists for all she knew. In general, they looked like Griffton people but she could be wrong. It was summer, so highly probable that visitors were being swept up in all this nonsense. Imagine coming to Griffton on holiday and finding yourself trapped as the apocalypse unfolded, she mused.

Iona laughed inappropriately when she saw the statue of Samyaza. It was most likely the shock of it, she reflected. The dark column was both surreal and sobering.

Instantly, the Dunamis rose up inside her, so strongly repelled by the evil monument that it made Iona feel physically sick. The reaction took her by surprise. But he was holy and pure and could not abide evil, she realised. All of a sudden, she comprehended the enormity of what was happening. The people were being weeded out. Those who follow the Rescuer from those willing to submit to Samyaza. And she knew she couldn't bow down in front of that thing. It was the end of the road.

"Oh Ben, this is awful," she said breathily. Her eyes tracked the height of the statue, starting from its lower third and eventually landing on the disfigured face of the dark angel.

"No, I don't like this at all." The statue was many times larger than the stone head that stood further along the cliff. Nobody talked about it anymore. It had done its job and just stood there uselessly now, near the oak tree at the edge of the cliff.

In comparison, the head was like a sapling compared to this great old yew tree, with its wide wings outstretched like branches. She couldn't see the bottom but it looked like they had kept the space around it clear of people. If it toppled forwards, it would most likely kill a thousand of them. Maybe that was their plan.

Ben held onto her tightly.

"We've got to get away from here," said Matt angrily. "If we could only get past those guards over there. That's where the forest starts, down the hill. I've been there before. It gets thick really fast. We could disappear. They'd never catch us."

"It's not going to be easy," said Ben. He nodded towards the sky. A cloud of black Angel Hunters was descending. They started circling the crowd slowly. Iona felt their eyes on her and the evil currents that floated her way.

"It's those things. They're everywhere," Iona exclaimed. "I've never seen them so close before." She shivered, the same way she did when she saw a big insect she didn't like. A fat cockroach or a furry moth.

"So, what now?" Grace asked.

"I don't know," answered Matt.

The guards made them shuffle forwards and directed them towards a field where they were told to wait. The grass had been flattened by a thousand shoes. It looked more like Astroturf than pastureland.

Iona stood tall and had a good look around her. She said excitedly, "Hey, isn't that Lake Emerson? Over there. Ben, look."

Ben peered into the distance. "Yes, I think so."

"His hair is white, like Rachel's," she commented. Then she lost sight of him.

"Did you see who he was with?"

Suddenly, an announcement sliced through the air and she forgot about Lake. It wasn't clear where it came from but everyone heard it clearly. The voice was androgynous but firm. Crisp and commanding.

"This is a public announcement. Stand by for your instructions."

There was silence for a while, which caused people to look at each other quizzically.

Then a second voice cut in. This one was deeper and more menacing. "You are here to pay respect to your lord and master, Samyaza. Your group will go forward to the idol in an orderly manner. You will bow or lie down before him. You will then be moved to your second location. There you will receive a gift from the master."

The voice stopped, and a stretch of quiet static ensued. It felt like the end of the announcement, which prompted a few people to start mumbling.

"Forget this," Matt said loudly. "I'm not doing it."

"Me neither," Ben insisted, adamantly.

People were starting to stir and dissent all around them, finding their voices at last. One tough guy even pushed a guard, only to be shoved back into the crowd. The guard showed him his gun. The big man toppled backwards and growled but stayed down.

"Worshipping Samyaza is mandatory," said the voice, as though it had read the mood of the crowd. "Samyaza is King. Samyaza is Lord. Samyaza will prevail."

"Like hell," said Matt. "I'm out of here." He moved slowly towards the border of the forest, pushing roughly through the crowds. All the while, he looked over his shoulder, checking above his head every so often. Sensing an opening between the guards, he started to run. The people happily let him through, cheering him on. They watched keenly for what might happen.

"Matt, be careful," Iona called after him. She felt overwhelmed by a sense of foreboding, but willed him to escape.

He almost reached the tree line when the voice said again, "Be advised: worshipping Samyaza is not optional." The announcer paused and then added, "Tel, Cam, Ti, Uz, Lo, Kom."

There was a series of dull-sounding explosions across the top of the cliff. Six in total. Two were nearby, the others further away. The mob fell into silence. Iona caught her breath, reluctant to believe her eyes. But she saw it all clearly.

Matt died at the tree line. Halted in his tracks. Caught in an explosion. The stark reality hit her. Matt was the explosion. It was the chip in the back of his neck. His new name, Kom. The announcer had called it out, ending his life. Each of those names was a person. A human being. A human bomb. Six lives gone. Just like that.

A chorus of screams pierced the air followed by frenzy then chaos. The people nearest Matt were the worst injured. She saw blood spattered across the faces of half a dozen of them. One was bleeding from the head and another had lost an arm. Another person was missing half of his jaw.

Iona fainted to the sounds of shrieking.

Chapter 36

"I don't want to do this, dad," Rory whispered to Daniel, after he stopped crying. "I don't want to bow in front of that thing."

"Nor do I," said Daniel, stony faced. "And there's no way they can make us. Samyaza can go jump off Griffton Cliff."

As soon as the bombs detonated in the distance, the group knew something terrible had happened. Rory felt the commotion that ensued lasted a long time. And then the screaming died down, although many people were still whimpering. Rory felt distressed to see so many men and women in tears.

The guards began to lead groups of people towards the Samyaza statue. They walked with heavy feet, reluctant to approach but yielding nonetheless. The Dream Fighters pushed them forwards and made them bow, kneel or lie down on the grass in front of the hundred-foot effigy. Meanwhile, the Dream Fighters began to chant in low tones: "Sor-cah-yah. Hom-kii-ta-ray. Who-par-key. Yor-way-mah." As they prostrated themselves, something happened in the hearts and spirits of the citizens. A dark, evil pressure fell on them, destroying their resolve, stealing their hope. It was a crushing, bending experience. And it was happening on a global scale.

Their minds convinced them this was the new order now. There were no choices - no options left. Everybody bows before Samyaza in the end. Samyaza is king, and he will prevail, their hearts told them. Survival was all they had left. And the only way to survive was to bow the knee to the king of the world. Only then would they have some assurance they would not die. There were no guarantees but at least, if they toed the line, they would be spared. And ultimately, everybody was doing it, which meant it was the right thing to do. The majority was always right, surely?

Rory shook his head in disbelief. He looked at the faces of his family and friends, Cameron, his mum, Caleb, Serena and Micah, and Lake. They all looked determined they would not be made to go forward.

"What do we do, Dad? How do we get away?"

Caleb asserted, "You know what we need to do, young Rory. We need to ask the Rescuer right away. We need to call on the Dunamis this minute. And remember, live or die, we win and the enemy loses. And your dad is right. There is no way that we are going over there to do what they're asking. It's not going to happen. Not today. Not ever."

Rory smiled. "Okay."

"So, grab hands. Everybody ready? Let's do this."

Together, they bowed their heads and closed their eyes.

Caleb said in a rich and commanding voice, "Mighty Rescuer, my King. My friend. Help. We need your help. Right now."

Everybody waited for him to go on, but he added, "That's it. That's all. Now we wait."

Rory opened his eyes and saw Caleb grinning. He liked the way he spoke simply and briefly. It was the way he talked to the Rescuer himself. Sometimes the simplest words have the greatest impact, he found.

There was a ruffling sound above. Looking up, he saw a flurry of white wings. The Warrior Angels had arrived. Hundreds of them. They swooped down from on high like streaks of lightning. Many of them pierced the black monsters with their swords. Rory fancied that he heard the quiet tune of the Protectors weaving through the air. The tide was turning. He saw one injured demon tumble out of the sky and smack into the ground. Another one toppled over the cliff and plummeted into the valley.

The Dream Fighter guards were thrown into confusion, roaring to each other and bellowing at the crowd to stay still. Nobody took any notice. People started to run in all directions. The guards were heavily outnumbered.

Daniel said quickly, "We need to get to the tunnel. The underground tunnel in the forest. Do you remember it?"

"No, not really," admitted Lake. "I was scared out of my mind, remember? I'd just escaped that lunatic Kumiko and her zombie Dream Fighter army!"

"Then stay close. And if we get split up, we meet there. Ask the Dunamis where it is."

"But they'll kill us if we try to escape," Lake panicked. "They've got guns. What do we have?"

"Stay calm, Lake."

"I'm trying."

Daniel shot back, "Try harder. The Rescuer is with you. Now. Here's our chance. Follow me. Keep up everyone."

He held Arabella's hand and made sure Rory and Cameron stayed close.

Taking advantage of the mayhem around them, they successfully darted into the trees. Rory saw Lake weave around a confused-looking Dream Fighter. It was like he was dribbling a ball and going on to score the winning goal in a football match. Nice footwork, he thought.

They ducked into the forest unhindered. But unfortunately, the bank was steep and Rory went over. Caleb scooped him up quickly and they kept going. Rory's knee was hurt but he didn't want to stop. He cried as he ran. Through the gaps in the branches, Rory glimpsed fighting in the sky above. Battles raged, the winged creatures silhouetted against a dark, cerulean-blue evening sky. Like sparks and ash rising high above a forest fire.

In that instant, a black Angel Hunter rocketed towards them through a gap in the trees, hurtling like a meteor. Rory let out a yelp.

Chapter 37

A blazing Warrior Angel halted the attacker mid flight, cutting it down with the edge of his sword. The angelic being paused in the air as his enemy fell to the ground behind Rory. Satisfied the group was safe, their protector raced back to battle, instantly becoming a streak of thick orange lightning.

The escapees carried on going. The trees thickened and they could no longer see the sky. Soon, the darkness of the woods surrounded them. They passed through a copse with hacked-down tree trunks at the centre. Bare and exposed, they looked to Rory like massive toadstool stems. The ground was springy and covered in twigs. Rory limped on, trying to keep up with the adults.

"That was close," said Micah, as they regrouped and checked on each other. They moved more slowly through the copse, feeling safer.

"How far, Dad?" Rory panted.

"Almost there."

Rory did a quick check to make sure everyone was together. Dad, Mum, Cam, Micah. Caleb, Serena.

He alerted his dad: "Lake! Where's Lake?"

"Sorry. We need to keep going."

"No!"

"Son, he'll meet us there."

"But he doesn't know where it is."

"I don't mean to be harsh but we must keep moving."

The forest quickly became dense, slowing their escape. It wasn't the way they'd come before, Rory realised. Also, he found it harder than the rest, being shorter and injured. Whereas they could leap over tall growths, he had to pick his way more carefully. In particular, he had to concentrate on staying upright and avoiding sharp bits of undergrowth. His knee was giving him more trouble with every step.

The tricky ground didn't last forever, though. Soon, they were descending more quickly. Thin trees whizzed past them and the hill levelled out.

It was a relief when they got to the tunnel entrance. Even better to discover that it didn't have Dream Fighters guarding it. On the contrary, it was just as they left it. There in the dark on that adventurous night. The night when the Zodiacs tried unsuccessfully to attack the house, and the Dream Fighters finished the job. Rory wondered if there was anything left of his and Cameron's bedroom. It was the first time in ages he'd really thought properly about their home.

They came to a stop, forming a circle around the trapdoor. Everyone listened hard. Rory could hear his own breathing and the dull noises far away up the cliff: shouting, movement. Lake had still failed to make an appearance. Rory looked around in all directions for him, peering into the forest.

"I'm really sorry, Rory. We can't wait for him here. We need to go in and hide. Check out the house. He knows where we are."

"But he doesn't, Dad."

"He's a smart man, my son. I brought him out of the house and this is where we came. So he does know where it is. He'll remember. Or he'll work it out. Don't worry."

Daniel opened the hatch and climbed in carefully, listening intently all the while. He used his phone for light to check the coast was clear. Satisfied that it was safe, he said to Arabella, "Come on darling, let's go home. And if the enemy is still in residence, they'd better stay out of my way."

Rory followed his brother and parents down into the hatch followed by Micah, Serena and, finally, Caleb, who had a light of his own.

Behind him, Rory heard Caleb saying, "Ah, Mr Emerson. Just in time! Would you kindly close that hatch behind you?"

Chapter 38

Rachel sat moaning softly on the floor in the corner of her room. The bed lay unmade to her left with the sink further along the wall and the toilet to the side. Sheets of paper, bearing Rachel's scribbled notes, were scattered beside her legs. Her uncapped pen was in the middle of the room where it had rolled to a halt. Like a stranded mariner adrift in the middle of the ocean. Stark light shone down but Rachel was unaware of it. She was somewhere else.

On her head was a lone Valenstriuccia, bobbing up and down leisurely. Doing violence to her mind. The wall behind propped up its blubbery body, supporting it as it unleashed its horrors. Its tentacles gripped her chin at the front and reached down her neck through her white hair.

Although Rachel's eyes were closed, she could see many things. She could see that there was glass in front of her face. At least, it seemed like glass. Clear and thick. A light snow brushed the windowpane. So pretty. Floating snowflakes. Dancing in the wind. Light and feathery. Sometimes they melted. Sometimes they stayed whole and stuck to the glass. Building up layers. The snowflakes got larger over time. Clumping together. It was peaceful. Like a cell phone background. One that moves in real-time. Or a relaxation video. It was as if she was watching a strange broadcast on a screen. If only it wasn't so chilly.

Gradually, the snowfall grew heavier, turning into a veritable blizzard. The white curtain of snow swished and floated before her eyes. So beautiful. She felt that she was still in Bhutan, in that frosty mountainous region. The place where she'd been kidnapped. She sensed she was alone. The others weren't with her. She knew this for certain.

As she stared at the snow falling against the window, she realised it wasn't a window after all. It was a thick sheet of ice. She was lying underneath it. Her face pressed up against it. Her nose almost touching. Her skin ached. She realised she was bitterly cold. A paralysing cold, in fact. She was floating underground. Completely immersed in freezing water. Trapped under ice. Panic rose up.

Rachel opened her mouth to scream. Painful water rushed in. It flooded her mouth and nose. Making her gag and choke. Her brain ached with the cold. There was a stabbing twinge in her lungs. Alarm. Pain. The agony of dying. It came on her by degrees, the drowning, which made her underwater death both painful and prolonged. It unfolded in slow motion, dragging her through each desperate second. Pulling her unwillingly through to the end, thrashing and kicking.

Eventually the scene faded, giving her a brief reprieve. But the Valenstriuccia's nightmare realm was only just beginning. It was merely getting acquainted: finding out about her. Probing for her deepest fears. Her greatest regrets. Investigating her anxious thoughts. Reaching into her memories and her dreams.

It found another juicy scenario to explore and forced her to walk the plank and plunge into it. In this one, Rachel was back in her cell. She could see herself from the outside. The scene chilled her. It was the horror of witnessing her own body: helpless and abandoned. She hated the feeling of being trapped. In a tiny room. With a monster. No escape.

Her legs stuck out perpendicular to the corner. One foot went straight up. The other was turned outwards. She saw a huge, grey, pulsating creature that engulfed her entire head. Eating her brain. It's tendrils reached down her body and attached themselves with hidden claws. She didn't love hats at the best of times, but this was a hat to beat them all. A revolting ogre of a hat. A torture hat. A sadistic, surreal hat.

It was close enough to reality to fill her with a sense of overwhelming dread. Was this what was really happening? It played on her mind. Was her head really engulfed by the monster? It might well be. So gross. In her mind, she knew she was being worn down, overpowered. And there was nothing she could do to stop it. For a girl who loved her freedom, this was utterly horrible. The worst kind of agony.

She felt physical pain as the creature bit repeatedly into her head. Like a surgeon, operating without any anaesthetic. Slicing at her nerve endings. Taking vital parts away. Bits of her brain that she needed to function. Although she couldn't see any teeth, because its mouth was hidden, she could feel them. They nicked her again and again. A swarm of hornets, stinging her head.

The Rachel in her mind tried to scream but was unable to express herself. She was defenceless. A rag doll. A victim. "Wake up Rachel. Fight!" her thoughts screamed. But the Rachel in front of her was fading fast. There was nothing she could do.

Suffocation followed. A slow and debilitating suffocation. Any hope she might have had, any faith in the Rescuer, was being crushed out of her. The Rescuer King wasn't around to save her. He wasn't around at all. He didn't care. He didn't exist. He didn't even feature in her thoughts. She was a stranger to him. And he was a fiction to her.

Finally, she succumbed to the Valenstriuccia's mistreatment. Everything blurred. Disintegrated. She fell from a great height as the scene darkened and shifted again. And as she plummeted, the enemy continued his relentless assault on her mind. Patiently and methodically picking through her thoughts. Delving deeper. Taking his time.

In the next dream, Rachel was standing on Griffton beach. Her senses confirmed it. Pebbly sand beneath her feet. Fresh salty air. Seagulls everywhere. Dive-bombing the shallow waves. Making that strange sound they make. "Squah! Squah!"

In her heart, she carried a certain level of anxiety that she would be pecked to death by birds at any moment. She was convinced it would be very slow and painful. But at present, the seagulls seemed content to search for food and leave her alone. Her sense of dread continued as she turned away from the beach to look at the buildings. The waterfront she knew so intimately. She prepared herself for the pleasant followed by the nasty. She was being tortured by the contrast. From the light down into the darkness.

Griffton was as she remembered. Only, it was intact in this vision. Just as it had been before the bombings and the riots. Pre-Samyaza. Suddenly, there was a screech to her right. A young woman appeared out of nowhere. Her hair was on fire: a blazing torch. The flames blackened her forehead. Burned her skin away. She tripped over, screaming.

Rachel sprinted over to help. But the woman thrashed her arms, attacking Rachel instead. She smacked Rachel painfully on the chest. Her clothes caught fire as Rachel watched. Tears of desperation came. It was horrible, seeing this stranger suffering. But she wouldn't let Rachel help her. She just kept batting her away.

She realised there was someone else nearby. Then she saw it. The Malkin.

It wandered leisurely along the beach towards her. Unhurried. Its white dress undulating in the breeze. Fixed expression. Robotic arms. One ended in a rounded stub. The other had five different fingers at the end. Rachel, Jia Li, Ndege, José and Paolo, she thought. My friends. Where are they? Are they also being tortured this way – lost in their own personal hell?

Rachel readied herself to run. "This is not happening," she told herself, desperately. But her mind was tired and her 'fight or flight' mechanism was beginning to kick in. She saw her mother's face in the distance, expressionless. "Not my mother," she told herself.

The Malkin continued to approach her. It definitely had her mother's eyes, which were exactly how she'd remembered them from being nine years old. Except these were cold and murderous. Vacant.

Turning to run, Rachel tripped over. She cut her arm on a broken rock as she fell. She got up again. Tumbled over again. Cut herself again. This time on a serrated shell. The Malkin was even closer now. What to do?

"I get it," thought Rachel. "There's no escape. It's time to die yet again." She glanced up at the Malkin's face and saw that it had turned into her own. Her big brown eyes. But with the same lifeless expression as before. A low, alien noise came out of its mouth.

Fear-drenched, Rachel froze as the Malkin bore down on her. The Malkin with her features. It pressed a fire-hot hand into her face. Covering her nose, her mouth and eyes. Scorching her flesh in the shape of a five-fingered hand. The index finger bisected her forehead. The little finger and thumb scored diagonal lines into her cheeks and eyes. There was a searing sensation that pulsed through her skin. It cut right through the muscles of her face and into her bones. The enemy had managed to brand her once again. The pain was excruciating.

The hellish burning lasted an age. The only relief she was given was the culmination of a sluggish, creeping death. When it came, Rachel was traumatised and exhausted.

But the Valenstriuccia was only starting to get into its stride. It had the energy and persistence of an industrial turbine. The cell door was locked. Nothing was going to shut it down.

Chapter 39

Ben held onto Iona's hand and pulled her through the crowd. She was so glad that her leg was healed and she could move freely. The screaming intensified as the demons swooped and the Dream Fighters began to fire indiscriminately at the people.

As she ran, Iona saw a citizen punch a Dream Fighter in the face. He was immediately hacked down with the edge of a sword, as the soldier swiftly retaliated. She skipped through the melee, her free hand clenched into a fist. Iona's mind could scarcely take in the warzone that had erupted around her. It was a scene of perpetual motion with danger literally everywhere. But, with Ben leading her, she just about managed to stay calm.

It was a miracle they were able to navigate through the chaos, waltzing successfully past the guards then racing down the slope towards the forest. It looked like the guards' eyes were temporarily blinded as they moved past them. Like they were invisible. Other people had the same idea but weren't so fortunate. Many were stopped gruesomely by swords or gunfire, which made Iona whimper and put her free hand over her ear.

Just before they reached the edge of the grassy plain, Iona glanced back. She saw a ring of black creatures descend. They fell heavily to the ground, like a black theatre curtain, and remained there. Together with the guards, they effectively cut off all escape routes and hemmed the crowd in. The enemy thereby plugged the leaks and regained control. However, they were still troubled by the Warrior Angels. These white-clad figures darted resolutely at the battle lines from above with drawn swords. Continually disrupting their adversaries. It was a highly dynamic scene, with arrows of light whizzing at their dark targets and then retreating, only to fly back again and again.

Ben and Iona ran on, determined not to stop until they found safety. She kept her eyes on the trees, running quickly and keeping two paces behind Ben who had finally let go of her hand. Clear at last, they hid themselves under the cover of the trees, crouching. He laid a protective arm around her shoulder. She peered nervously around them, flicking her wild hair away from her face. The trunks and branches protected them from diving demons and firing guards for the time being.

"Let's keep moving," Ben rasped, having caught his breath. Iona nodded. They didn't know where they were heading. But they felt for certain that anywhere would be better than up on the cliff.

"I think there's an old farmhouse this way," said Ben. "But I'm not sure."

"Doesn't matter," Iona replied. "Just don't leave me."

"Never," shot Ben, staring into the distance.

Despite the circumstances, Iona managed to smile.

°°°°°*12345*°°°°°

Slowly and with some apprehension, Daniel pushed open the secret trapdoor. It led into his study via the fireplace. His room would be the perfect place from which to run a dictatorship, he imagined. He envisaged the enemy using his walls to chart their attacks, plot their schemes and dominate the world. His desk would be the place where Samyaza would do his best work: brutalising and destroying buildings and lives. Terrorising all of creation.

He peered anxiously over the threshold, ready to see a room full of Dream Fighters or worse. Instead, he immediately saw that the coast was clear. Nothing stirred. The lights were off but there was still some daylight outside which illuminated the room.

His study smelled musty: un-aired. He was relieved to see it was largely intact. There were piles of books on the floor. His books. His desk was untidy. Apart from that, he didn't see many other things out of place. While this was a relief, he doubted the rest of the house looked this good. He hated to think what might have happened to Arabella's dresser or their en suite bathroom. The demonic hordes are not known for their cleanliness, after all. He'd find out soon enough.

"I'm going up," he whispered to the others.

He hauled his body through the hole. Brushed the dust off his knees. Snatched up a poker from the wrought-iron tool holder at the side. Then he paced around quietly, holding his breath. At the door of the study he listened hard, calming his breathing and straining his ears. There were few noises in the house. The ticking of an antique clock several rooms away. The quiet hum of a fridge.

As the others emerged from the secret passage, he switched on the power to the control centre. He was relieved that it worked straight away. Arabella came and stood by his side as he settled himself into his leather study chair. It was as comfortable as ever. He relaxed a little, spreading his legs. His wife put her hand on the back of his neck.

"What's next, Dan?"

"Can we check our room?" Cameron enquired.

"Not yet, son. Stay put. Let me have a look around using the cameras. Then we'll check the whole house together. Make sure no one's lurking around. Caleb, could you stand at the door?"

Caleb nodded and took up his position, ready to lay out a guard if necessary. Either with his fists or the power of the Dunamis, whatever felt best.

Daniel's computer booted up and he switched on a line of three flat screens. Seconds later, they were filled with CCTV images. Lake, Serena and Micah looked on with interest. Arabella and the boys had seen it all before, so decided to wait on the floor in the corner. Arabella sat in the middle and held one hand each. Rory fidgeted as he waited. "I'm hungry," he whispered.

"We'll get something soon," she replied kindly.

As Daniel flicked through the security cameras, he saw that the house was in a dire state: trashed to within an inch of its life. The best news was there were no Dream Fighters anywhere to be seen. Unless they were hiding, which was unlikely. It wasn't really their style. No Angel Hunters either, which was a relief to everyone. And no Samyaza for that matter: an even bigger mercy. In fact, there was no movement at all, which was a mystery.

"It looks like the enemy has moved on," Daniel declared. "I can't see anyone on the roof, outside, or on any of the floors. The bedrooms are clear, as far as I can see. So are the function rooms, the kitchen and the basement. And also the watchtower on the drive. What do you think, Arabella? Caleb?"

"We need to be sure," said Arabella.

"It would be good to search the house," agreed Caleb. "But we must be careful. There might be a trap or an ambush. I wouldn't put it past Samyaza. Could he have sabotaged your camera equipment so everything looks clear?"

Daniel furrowed his brow and checked again. "Let me check the feeds and the times. Give me a second while I zoom in on the grandfather clock in the hall. No, we're okay, this is real. We're seeing what we're seeing."

"Okay then. I think we should search the house, but very carefully," said Caleb.

"We're agreed then. My preference would be to start from the front, make sure the doors and windows are locked. We should stick together and work backwards. How does that sound?"

"Sounds okay dad. But could we maybe start from the kitchen?" asked Rory.

"Why is that, monkey?" Daniel queried.

"Well, I'm starving." Rory smiled.

"All right," Daniel laughed. We'll search the house from the front, but detour via the kitchen. See if the enemy has left us anything to eat."

"Thanks Dad," Rory smiled.

Chapter 40

Incredibly, the fridge and cupboards were full to overflowing with food and drink. There were fizzy drinks, much to the children's delight, and even some bread. It was a little stale, though, which indicated to the group that the enemy had possibly vacated the premises several days ago. They also found some fruit and vegetables, and even some cheese and butter in the fridge.

"So, while the rest of Griffton is struggling to feed themselves, Samyaza makes sure his crew is all right," Caleb commented.

"How like a dictator. He's such a cliché," said Lake.

"It's as much as you would expect," said Daniel. He added, "Right, everyone ready? Have you had enough to eat for now? We really should search this place."

Rory smiled, and asked politely, "Are we allowed any dessert?" Serena giggled, grabbing Caleb's hand.

Arabella answered him, "Okay, why don't you and Cam see what you can find in the larder? I think I saw some chocolate biscuits in there, believe it or not."

"All right, but no more delays. Bring them with you and let's make sure this place is safe."

Armed with a pack of chocolate biscuits, the group moved forwards to the front of the house. They walked back past Daniel's study, through the base of the stairwell and over to the entrance hall. Arabella gasped as she saw the rip in the painting of the Prince Regent and his horse. There were scuff marks on the walls and floor, as though people had been wrestling each other.

Outside the front door, everything was quiet. Daniel could see that the gates at the end of the long driveway were shut. The octagonal keep sat in solitude, and nothing could be seen through the windows. Caleb and Serena volunteered to have a look around, just to be sure.

Meanwhile, Daniel, Micah and Lake wandered around the driveway. Arabella and the boys stayed at the front door, her arms folded across her chest as she watched them all nervously. Daniel checked behind the row of lime trees. Micah investigated both sides of the house. There was a lot of evidence of soldier activity. Spent ammunition, building materials, broken pots. But nobody was home.

They re-entered the mansion and locked the doors. This time they chose to walk through the left hand side of the house. The drawing room, dining room and billiard rooms were clear. And so was the Orangery beyond it. Again, shattered glass, broken ceramics and scuff marks abounded. There were some noxious items left behind in the Orangery as well, a thick jelly the colour of mustard and some rancid apples. They circled back through the kitchen, where Daniel decided it was safe to leave Arabella and the boys, who were hungry again.

"Caleb, Serena, Micah and Lake, are you okay to check the top floor with me? Then we'll do the middle. It's probably better if Arabella doesn't see the master bedroom!"

"Do you know what? It's all just stuff at the end of the day," said Arabella firmly. "If they've trashed my Egyptian cotton and ruined my towels, I'll obviously be disappointed. But it's all just stuff after all. Besides, I would rather stay here with the boys and enjoy a quiet cup of tea."

"Good plan, Bella."

"And besides, you're right. I don't want to see what they've done to our home."

"Is it okay if I stay here too?" asked Lake.

Daniel raised his eyebrows.

"I mean, I like your house and everything. But it's got some bad memories for me, if you know what I mean?"

"Oh, you mean the time you worked for the enemy?"

"Yeah, that kind of thing." Lake shuffled from foot to foot.

Daniel smiled. "That's okay. I used to work for him too, as you know. No, that's fine, Lake. It's all in the past now. Forgiven and forgotten. You stay here and help Arabella keep an eye on the kids."

"Great, we can have a drink and play Yahtzee," said Rory, delightedly.

"That's settled then. We'll meet back here and then whoever wants to can check out the basement with me."

"That's where they used to have their gatherings," Lake shivered.

"What do you mean?" asked Micah.

"He means, it's where they used to summon Samyaza. Before he came back to the earth," Daniel explained. "I know far too much about the old rituals. More than I should. It feels like decades ago though."

"Yes, you're a new man now. Never forget that," said Caleb. "Right, before we go, let's have a chat with the Rescuer. We should ask his help and protection."

"Yes, that's a good idea," agreed Serena. "I feel the Dunamis would say that the house is clear, but that something unexpected is coming. We need to be on our guard."

"Do you think they'll come down from Griffton Cliff?" Cameron asked. "They are pretty close after all. And they know this house."

"I don't know. Stay sharp everyone though," said Caleb. Then he added, "Cameron, why don't you ask the Rescuer for his help this time? On our behalf."

Cameron nodded. After a while, he quietly said, "Dear Rescuer, please will you help us search this house? Keep us safe. Protect us from the enemy."

"Nice and simple. Does the job," said Caleb. He turned to Daniel. "Lead on," he commanded gruffly.

"Right then. Caleb, Serena, Micah, let's go," Daniel said. He led them out to the stairs.

°°°°°°*12345*°°°°°°

Twenty minutes later, Daniel marched a sheepish-looking Kumiko down the stairs and into the kitchen. She smelled of shampoo and body wash and her hair was wrapped in a pink towel. She was in a baggy grey T-shirt, pink shorts and bare feet.

"You?" Lake said accusingly.

"Hey, Lakie. I thought you'd be glad to see me." She smiled wearily, rubbing the towel against her hair on one side.

Lake roared, "Don't trust anything she tells you. She's a liar."

Kumiko quietly unravelled the towel, revealing a mass of long, straight white hair. Lake stood and stared.

"Look, she's even dyed her hair white to pretend she's one of us." Lake fumed. "Nothing is beyond her."

Kumiko stood and sighed. She didn't argue back. Arabella marvelled at her lengthy, bright white hair and the boys hung back, unsure about how they should react.

"She didn't put up a fight," said Caleb, calmly.

"Course she wouldn't. She's a coward. And she's outnumbered," Lake declared. "She's a criminal. Worse than a criminal. She sided with Samyaza. Fought with him. For him. She's the enemy. And she destroyed Rachel's house. She's the reason Eddie's dead. The reason the Griffton News got burnt down. And I can't forgive you." He started sobbing.

Kumiko stood quietly, her head bowed.

After a long while, Caleb said, "She told us she met the Rescuer. Says he's forgiven her. Forgiven her for everything. Changed her heart." Lake was shaking his head.

"And I believe her," Caleb continued. He directed that last phrase at Lake. "I believe her," he said again, softly.

"And so do I," said Serena. "The Rescuer's paid for her. That means he owns her now. And she carries his Dunamis. She's

176

renounced Samyaza. We talked to her upstairs."

"Lake, he nearly killed me," Kumiko said gently. "And I am sorry. So sorry I hurt you. Sorry for everything. If I could take it all back; start again…"

Lake closed his eyes and breathed deeply. "You met the Rescuer?" he asked.

"Yes. He's beautiful. Like no one I've ever met before."

"Okay," said Lake, simply. "If he's forgiven you; well…" He looked at her, calm now. She looked like a different person. Not shadowy and secretive like before. Her eyes were clear and there was nothing hidden in her face. In fact, she looked like a young girl, innocent and fresh. And then there was that freaky hair: white like his. White to the roots. She held his gaze, looking at him imploringly.

"If he's forgiven you, then, I guess, so can I. I forgive you Kumiko. For everything."

"Just like that?" She smiled, looking quizzical.

"Yes. Just like that. But don't ever ask me to write for you again." He grinned.

"It's a deal, boy."

Everybody relaxed.

"Good then. Now listen up everyone. There's something you all need to know," said Kumiko. She instantly had everyone's attention.

"I saw where they went. I can take you there."

Chapter 41

The nine of them stood in the basement, staring in awe at the green-tinged rift. It hung in the air, lightning shaped: a spectral mist. Every so often, it flickered like a gossamer wing.

Rory wandered around the back of it and commented, "Hey, you can't see it from the other side! All you can see is you guys and a messy storeroom. But when you come back round, you can see it in the air. Like Christmas tinsel. It's amazing. Like those rocks in the mezzanine. The ones that just hang there in the air and sometimes they disappear."

"They left through here," said Kumiko. "Some of the Dream Fighters from the house. Not that I saw them exactly. But I know a few went back into the house, and the rest went up to the cliff. I heard them going down into the basement. I was hiding. And they didn't come back. My theory is they didn't want to stick around after the Rescuer appeared on the scene."

"He was here?" asked Daniel.

"Sure. But not for long. He fixed me up. Then he went away. Then everyone else left."

"Okay. And as far as you know, has anyone returned?"

"Nobody. I check on it every so often. It just hangs there like that. The house has been empty for a few days. They're restless, you know. They like to move on. Like locusts."

Kumiko continued, "This is the room where they used to come and try and talk to him, you know. In this room. But I could hear him directly myself. He was in my head. In my heart. And all those years, he was watching me." She shuddered.

She carried on rambling, as if to herself, "And in the end, he wasn't who I thought he was. No, he was far worse than anything I could ever imagine. He's a monster, inside and out. And he used me."

"Could Samyaza have taken Rachel through there?" mused Serena. "Back into the mezzanine? That's got to be where it leads, right?"

Kumiko said, "Yes. More than likely. He's always been obsessed with that girl. But who really knows with him?"

Caleb put his hand up against the rift. Small sparks of electricity flew off but didn't burn him. He put his fingertips up to it and they passed through, disappearing. As he pulled his hand back, he was relieved to see it was still in one piece. "We need to go in. There's nothing to fear. The Dunamis is with us."

Unexpectedly, Kumiko started pleading, "I'm coming, yeah? Don't leave me here. Please. I need to be part of this. Stopping Samyaza, I mean. If it's even possible. Will you let me help?"

Daniel and Caleb looked at each other and then at Arabella and Serena.

"I'm fine with it," asserted Lake, though no one had asked him.

"The more the merrier," Caleb grinned. "Everyone coming? Micah, Daniel, Arabella, kids?"

"Well, I'm certainly not staying behind and letting Daniel go on his own. It was hard enough when the enemy took Rory. When Cameron and I had to go through to the island without them. The waiting was almost more than I could bear. And I would prefer not to leave the children here, considering everything that's going on at the top of Griffton Cliff. In my opinion, either we all go or we all stay," Arabella said firmly.

"I'm up for it," said Cameron quickly. "I mean, it's great to be home. And all our stuff's here and everything. But we need to see if we can find Rachel. She's our friend. And some things are more important than stuff."

Rory added, "I like adventures. Even dangerous ones. I'm happy to come as well. But, if it's okay with you all, I need to do a loo stop first."

"Yes, of course young man," said Caleb. "That's sound advice for us all. Anyone else need the toilet before we go? Serena?"

Serena slapped him on the arm and screwed up her face.

Chapter 42

Rachel was having a nightmare about Lake, although it started off well enough. It was a balmy evening. The predominant colours were yellow and orange, and even the sea was tinged with turmeric tones.

They were sitting on a wooden bench by the sea, eating chocolate ice cream. Lake was on her right hand side, making her laugh. He looked handsome and was being very attentive to her, which she liked. She realised she missed him a lot.

But very soon, she became aware that Kumiko was sitting on her left, stock-still like a mannequin. She was wearing her signature pink and stank of vanilla perfume. Lake started smiling at her across Rachel and winking. This went on for a long time and made her feel incredibly awkward. Eventually, Lake ignored Rachel completely and started chatting exclusively with Kumiko. First it was annoying, then it was gutting.

Soon, without any warning, Lake and Kumiko stood up and grabbed one of Rachel's arms each. What happened next was shocking and Rachel endured a slow and horrible death as the two of them mauled her mercilessly. The physical torture lasted an untenably long time, with much pain and blood loss. But, tired though she was, she decided to receive the wounds to her body and her heart stoically.

In this way, she wearily succumbed to the Valenstriuccia's sadistic pleasures. Death approached slowly, washing her down its plughole like a sink full of dirty water. She slipped into the darkness once again and awaited the next horror.

In the subsequent dream, she was back in Bhutan, being grabbed by Dream Fighters. She felt alone in the cold and unfriendly terrain, without her dad or Lake. She bounced along, slumped over the shoulder of a big man, freezing by degrees. Bundled into a sack like a harvest of potatoes, she suffocated to death in the bowels of an aeroplane.

As the hum of the engine and the dark sacking fabric faded, Rachel felt weary to the point of death. But she knew the enemy wouldn't let her duck out of life. Samyaza was not that merciful.

The next scenario was incredibly cruel. She stood in her kitchen aged nine. The cupboards and surfaces were all how they used to be. It was a patchwork of pale yellows and beige, probably quite hideous, though Rachel liked it as a young girl.

A few years after this, her dad saved up the money to redo the kitchen. He installed it himself though it took a long time to complete. The problem was he was either out doing other jobs or drinking himself into oblivion.

In the kitchen, her mother was gasping for breath, her eyes massive, rolling. Rachel had lived this a thousand times already throughout her childhood. At night. In quiet moments. Waiting for a bus. The memory usually came to her unannounced. Her mother was wearing an apron over her dress: the one with large pink and orange flowers. White patches of flour covered the front because they had been making chapatis together. Her own hands were floury and white. Eddie was out at work as usual. And her mum had collapsed without any warning in the middle of the kitchen. Did it really happen like this? Yes, this is how it happened, more or less.

Young and helpless, she grabbed onto her mother, screaming, weeping. Seconds later, she would run to the neighbours, but it would be too late.

Why was the enemy putting her through this? She'd already lived it from every angle, with every emotion and outcome. Was there anything left in this memory to torture her with? She'd done all the 'what ifs' and played them over in her head.

In the alternative realities, her dad had come home to the rescue. Or her mum had revived and hugged her close. Or she discovered life-saving first aid skills she never knew she had. An ambulance just happened to be passing by, which rushed her to hospital and saved her life. Or it had been a prank and they laughed together uncontrollably afterwards.

Surely she had sucked everything out of the incident? Didn't the enemy know there was nothing more to be gained? Nothing to see here. She'd died a thousand times along with her mother. She'd hated herself to death for years for being so useless. She hated her father for being out at work, and then for not coping with the loss. And then recently, she'd gained her new perspective. An outlook that changed everything. She had forgiven herself and trusted the whole desperate mess to the Rescuer. And he took away her pain. He flushed her clean with fire; renewed her completely: inside and out. And he turned her hair white. That's right. Her hair was white now, not black like it used to be.

She suddenly became conscious that the Rescuer was standing right there with her in the kitchen. She thought she saw his face, only dimly, like in a dusty mirror. Eyes of compassion. Eyes of love. Was he real? She wasn't sure. She felt her heart growing warm as she sensed his presence. Just for a few seconds. Nothing lasting.

Then her dead mother sat up and choked her to death, staring at her like a ghoul. The Valenstriuccia had reasserted control. There was no hope here, only treachery and death. Rachel expired slowly at the hands of her mother. But she was certain she'd seen the Rescuer. He was with her. Just as he'd promised. Something stirred deep within her. Hope.

Chapter 43

While the others got ready, Lake had a few minutes alone with Kumiko down in the basement.

"What happened after I left? Escaped, I mean."

"I was so angry with you. I remember that. And I did things. Horrible things. I was horrible. A monster, like him. When I think about it, it's like I was somebody else. Someone I don't recognise. I hurt people, Lake. And destroyed things."

"Rachel's house? The Griffton News?"

Kumiko hung her head. "Yeah. And a lot more besides."

"These are crazy times," said Lake, kindly. "Crazy times," he fixed his eyes on the rift. "So what happened to you? How did you meet him? The King?"

"Samyaza hurt me, Lake. I thought he was going to kill me. He threw me against the wall, can you believe it? I broke some bones. Crawled outside onto the drive. The Rescuer found me there. It was incredible, Lake. He took away the pain, like completely. Fixed up my body. I think he did something inside that changed me, in my mind or my emotions, I don't know." Kumiko had tears in her eyes. "It's hard to explain."

Lake nodded.

"Me of all people, imagine. He gave me a fresh start. Boy, did I need a new start. I messed up big time. I am so thankful to him."

"You and me both."

Kumiko laughed. "He even gave me a new name, can you

believe it?"

"Go on then, what is it?"

"Well, you know how my name's Kumiko Starkweather?"

"Sure."

"Well, he calls me Kumiko Fairweather."

"That's cute," Lake smiled.

"Well, I am pretty cute," she agreed.

The others started to come down the stairs and into the storeroom.

"Are we ready?" Caleb asked in a booming voice.

Eight heads nodded at him.

"Great. Then let's go and end this."

°°°°°*12345*°°°°°

The sun was setting over Griffton, pressing the city towards darkness. Up on the cliff, the dark forces were back in command. Warrior Angels took their opportunities where they could, felling a Dream Fighter or wounding an Angel Hunter. These victories were few and far between, however.

The angels' strength relied on the faith and hopes of the humans, which was currently waning. The enemy had added a pack of spectral cats to their army. Exotic and feral, these panthers, lions and tigers encircled the people, keeping them in check. The crowds watched them warily, reluctant to make any sudden moves.

As they were brought over, wave upon wave of citizens fell before the statue, giving themselves to Samyaza. The Dream Fighters chanted incessantly, providing an odd kind of background music. Bass-heavy and monotonous. Many people wept and wailed, and this was acceptable to the enemy overlords.

Regardless, whether they came forward willingly or under duress, it mattered little to Samyaza. His primary objective was to subdue mankind and wring out whatever praise and glory he could. As far as he was concerned, sitting on his throne in his mezzanine citadel, victory was victory regardless of how it came about.

Griffton was a microcosm of what was happening across the globe. Statues of Samyaza took pride of place in Washington, Tokyo, Sydney, Beijing and London. They stood proud in Islamabad, Berlin and Paris. Rome, New York, Ottawa and Athens had statues of their own.

In some cities, Dream Fighters marched triumphantly alongside massive demons, Grigori comrades of Samyaza. And like their leader, they struck fear into the hearts of anyone who looked at them, so malformed and hideous were they.

In other places, they were accompanied by stunningly-beautiful Nephilim creatures, the deadly offspring of the fallen ones. Unpredictable and violent, they raged around, attacking people at random.

In every location, an oppressive gloom blanketed the proceedings. Stifling the free will of the people. It was Samyaza's day of triumph. A dark day on earth.

Chapter 44

Rory found himself standing on a rocky promontory, surrounded by pale pink water. Stepping through the green doorway in the basement of Lytescote Manor was a similar experience to going through the stone head, he found. Both journeys ended up in the mezzanine, with its purple and magenta sky colouring everything around.

Despite Rory being prepared for the mezzanine experience, he was still wowed by it. This time his senses worked straight away without needing to adjust. A gentle wind blew: a warm summer breeze. The water moved slowly: its tips flecked with purple. The grass they stood on was also on the purple scale with a few dollops of ultramarine here and there. Even their clothing took on plum hues, particularly if you were wearing white. The sounds in the air were unusual and slightly menacing. There was a crackle and a hissing that he hadn't heard before.

Looking around, Rory quickly ascertained that his parents and Cameron and Micah had come through all right. He relaxed, remembering the time when Rachel had ended up somewhere else in the mezzanine. That happened the first time they came through.

Caleb and Serena were holding hands further up the peninsula. Lake, standing beside Kumiko, watched as she gazed intently at everything, swaying like a drunk: striving to keep her balance. Rory realised this was her first trip to the mezzanine.

"It's all right," he called over to her. "You feel wobbly at first but you get used to it after a while."

"Can you feel anything? The ground or the wind?"

"Not really. I feel a bit like a ghost, floating."

"Like I said, the feeling goes away after a while."

Kumiko looked at him and raised her eyebrows. "What is this place?" she asked, incredulously.

"They call it the mezzanine," Lake commented. "I felt the same way about it when I first came through. Took me a while to get used to it."

"You've been here before?"

Lake nodded. "Just be on your guard. Things aren't always as they seem."

"What do you mean?"

"There are things here. Things that belong to Samyaza. Bad things. Like the sort of company you used to keep. But there are also good things about the mezzanine as well. You just need to keep your eyes open."

"Will do, cowboy."

Rory noticed the water was moving more slowly now, thickening. Gradually it became like wine-red custard. And then it solidified, going an even darker shade. Rory touched it with his foot. Firm ground. He stepped onto it, making an impression with his trainer.

"Hey, look at this everyone!"

"Please be careful," said Arabella.

Rory stepped back, in obedience. "It's okay. I think it's okay to walk on."

"I'm not so sure. Why don't we stick to the bit we're already on? We haven't fallen through that yet."

"Okay," Rory agreed. At the edge of the headland was the portal back to the basement of Lytescote Manor, shimmering in the air. It was a thing of beauty.

Rory turned back round and saw there were two figures standing beyond Caleb and Serena. They were up the slope, where the ground widened and became the mainland. It stretched out to the left and right, undulating into the distance. Rory saw that the figures were white and tall, instantly recognisable as angels. He gawped at the now-familiar flashing garments and marvelled. They waited patiently, the breeze ruffling their wings.

Caleb walked up to them, saying simply, "Hello."

"I am Gavreel," said one of them in a loud, clear voice. "We saw you coming through."

"I am Ramiel," said the other. "Follow us. Quickly. You are in danger."

"Angels?" Kumiko queried.

"Yes," said Lake. "Neat, aren't they?"

The tall creatures began walking up the hill at a pace. Caleb and the others were forced to follow. However, the group found it hard to keep up. Particularly the boys who were just getting used to their mezzanine legs. Nevertheless, they realised there was a sense of urgency and trotted along.

"Do you know where our friend Rachel is?" Rory called out. But the angels either ignored or hadn't heard him. "Did the Rescuer send you?" he continued.

"What is the nature of the danger? Tell me." Caleb asked forcefully. He strode behind the guardians.

"Come this way. It's not far."

"You can tell us. We come from Griffton where the enemy is pressing the people to worship Samyaza. He has tightened his grip and there is no safety there. What kind of danger are we in here? Tell us, servants of the Rescuer."

But the angels continued to ignore Caleb. They looked forwards and remained silent. "Where are you taking us?" He tried again. No reply was forthcoming.

He fell behind and walked with the others.

"Caleb, I don't know about this," said Daniel quietly. He held Arabella's hand as he walked. "It doesn't feel right to me."

"I agree," said Serena softly. "I have a bad feeling."

"They're not very nice," Rory observed. "Not like the other

189

ones we met."

They came to the top of a hill which overlooked an expansive valley. Clumps of black trees rose up from the basin. The ground itself was copper coloured with brick-red patches here and there. In the far distance a range of squat, black mountains spanned the horizon.

Rory thought he saw shadows move between the trees in the valley. He squinted, trying to make them out. It was possible his eyes were playing tricks on him. After all, he reasoned, things appear and disappear all the time in the mezzanine.

"Down there," said Gavreel. "We must make haste. Come." The lofty angel started to move forwards.

"Are there more of you down there?" Caleb questioned.

"No. But you will find safety there. We need to hurry. Come, let's…"

He stopped speaking as two streaks of lightning shot down to the ground. One was ruby red, the other amethyst purple. As they hit the ground, they transformed into two brilliant white angels. In an instant, Rory saw them open their wings and draw their swords. They wore shining tunics and their whole bodies rippled with light. A radiant glow flashed across their drawn swords. In comparison, the other two figures seemed dull and grey.

"Stand back," commanded one of the new arrivals. His voice was rich and melodic. "There's an ambush ahead."

Seconds later, the two new angels cut down the first two. Their clothes immediately faded and they were revealed as the shape shifters they were. Pale, grey and wretched, just like Zed. Cursing and screaming, they collapsed to the rocky ground and eventually lay still, lifeless. Rory stared at them, his eyes huge.

"The enemy likes to masquerade as angels of light," explained one of the angels. "Even on earth. We need to leave this place. It isn't safe here for any of us."

Daniel spoke rapidly: "Why didn't they try to kill us?"

"They knew they were outnumbered. You have great power."

"Yes that's right. The Dunamis is with us," Rory declared.

"Also, the Protectors war on your behalf."

Rory smiled, remembering the honour of activating his Protector on the reef.

"Do you know where Samyaza dwells?" asked Caleb.

"We do. It isn't safe there either. But we are tasked with taking you there and accompanying you into the fortress. Rachel Race is being held there with the four. Together, we will face the enemy. So be strong and very courageous, and the Rescuer will prevail."

"How do we get to the fortress?" asked Caleb.

"We need to travel underground to get to the enemy's citadel. Our army is attacking it from above as we speak. We will approach from beneath. The way to the caves is through that forest."

"Caves," said Caleb. He furrowed his brow.

The group allowed themselves to be led down the hill to the right. They didn't go down into the valley where the shadows played. Instead, they wove their way into a dark blue forest. Rory was comforted by this. He felt much safer amidst the trees than out in the open.

"We trust them, don't we?" Arabella checked with Daniel. "They seem different from the others. More like the ones we've met in the past."

"Yes, we trust them."

Caleb and Serena nodded in agreement.

As they went, Rory asked a series of big questions. "Hey Angel, is it going to be dangerous where we're going?"

"Yes. Dangerous for you. Dangerous for us. The enemy is relentless."

"What happens if you die in the mezzanine?"

"We are spirit beings. If we die, we return to the Rescuer. He has the power to send us back here or to earth as he chooses. After that, we are at his bidding and your service."

"So, what happens to us? If we die here? Does the same thing happen?"

"You are not like us. You are spirit and flesh, Rory. If you die

191

here, your body dies but your spirit will go to be with the Rescuer. There's no coming back. But if you do find yourself at that point, take heart and don't fear death."

Chapter 45

Gnarly, majestic trees stood shoulder to shoulder all around. They looked so different from the forest on the side of Griffton Cliff. That was tame in comparison. The trees here had broad and elongated arms that looked like trunks themselves. They hung in the air, their branches interwoven like tendrils.

Rory saw an electric-blue creature scurry across the bark of one tree. The surface was a shade of blue so dark it almost looked black. Underfoot, the path was uneven with bumpy roots and twigs.

Also, if you didn't pay attention, Rory discovered, it was easy to get hit in the face by a vine growing at head height. But whenever this happened, he found them soft, like feather dusters. They tickled his face instead of giving him a black eye. Because of this, he and Cameron actively sought them out, so they could have their faces stroked.

Cameron noticed a plant that looked like a red lollipop. It was round and flat like an oversized coin. He picked up one of the stems and annoyed Rory by pretending to lick it, coming right up close to his face.

"Hey! Stop doing that Cam!"

"Oh, come on. Why don't you try one?"

"You're not actually licking it are you? It could be poisonous!"

"Nah, don't be silly."

They travelled through the forest side-by-side. One angel took the lead and one followed at the rear, keeping watch. Caleb and Serena trod behind the Warrior Angel at the front. After them came Daniel and Arabella, with Micah and the kids behind. Lake and Kumiko walked quietly towards the back. The angels warned everyone to stay vigilant.

Rory listened in as a conversation started up behind him. It was one of the great things about being a kid: people don't know when you're tuning in. Often, it isn't even on their radar, thought Rory.

"We're all right, you and me, aren't we?" asked Kumiko.

"Of course we are. Why do you ask?"

"You know."

"Water under the bridge."

"When we find her, don't let her hate me. You'll say something, won't you?"

"She's not going to hate you, Kumi. Rachel's changed as well since she met the Rescuer. She's different. You'll see."

"You will talk to her though, in case? Sheesh, I burnt down the girl's house. If I were her…"

"I know. But a lot's changed since then. The whole world's different now."

"Yeah. I guess it is. No thanks to me."

"Kumi, it's water under the bridge. There are things far more important than playing the blame game. We need to try and change the way things are. That's what matters. And if we don't, it's all over."

Eventually, the forest thinned out. The angel in front pointed out the entrance to the caves. It was made of black rocks, with a mouth high enough to walk into with room to spare.

Soon, they were wading ankle-deep in cold water. Rory found the cave floor slippery and had to concentrate to keep his balance. He tripped over a couple of times and got his hands wet trying to right himself. In the end, Micah decided to take responsibility for him and hold his hand.

"You're all right, young man," said Micah, smiling. "Easy

there."

The sides of the caves glowed gently, illuminated by the angels' garments and swords. Rory noticed that the light was predominantly white in nature. But at the front, the black rock glowed with a reddish tinge. And looking back, he could see the cave walls assume a light purple colour. He pointed this out to his brother, who nodded and grinned.

"Like light sabres," Cameron commented.

"Cool," agreed Rory.

He was relieved that they were now walking on dry ground and the caves were wider in this section.

The angel in front gathered them together and spoke. "We need to climb upwards from here." He indicated a shaft that was ribbed with handholds. It ascended into darkness which flickered with light a long way up.

"Very soon, we will be underneath the enemy's citadel. We have created a route into the fortress. We will join our companions at the entrance and go in together. They are waiting for us at the top of this tunnel. Remember, your faith is our fuel. Let us do the fighting. And the Dunamis be with us all."

Without further delay, he began to climb. As he travelled upwards, he lit the rungs, deep indents in the walls, each of which were a foot wide. They rose up further than they could see. Rory realised they had a long and difficult climb ahead of them. After that, who knew what danger lay ahead in the citadel?

Chapter 46

In the next nightmare scenario, the creature placed Rachel in a circular pool, reminiscent of a stone cauldron. The sort that cannibals use in the cartoons to cook their guests. Throw in some carrots and potatoes and your Rachel Soup is complete, she thought. Anyone got any salt and pepper?

At first, it wasn't unpleasant, despite an underlying feeling that everything was about to go bad. She saw that the pool was at the centre of a darkened cave, where it was impossible to see very far. There were definitely some vampire bats in the corners, she envisaged.

However, the sound of the lapping water eased away some of the pain of her previous nightmares and her most recent death. That one was slow and painful like many of the others. It centred on a cloud of revolting African Hornets. They had huge black bodies and spiky orange mandibles. And they were merciless, stinging and stabbing her over and over again. All over her head, body and limbs. How she hated them. Wherever they injected their poison, her skin swelled up. Death came as a relief, painful though it was.

In this latest dream, it was almost like the water was sent to soothe her. Heal her sores and the places where the stings had entered. She was determined to make the most of it: her moments of respite. But then, just as she had expected, the scene started to change.

The water stirred deep down below. She felt the beginnings of a vortex emerging in the depths. A tidal pool. The current would no doubt drag her under and drown her any second. The enemy would most likely make her drown slowly and painfully again. It would be in a way designed to crush her resolve. Steal her hope. Or else, she would be dashed repeatedly against a jagged floor of hidden rocks. It would tear her flesh and make her suffer. The routine was becoming both tedious and predictable, which may perhaps be the enemy's plan. Maybe they were trying to bore her to death through repetition, agonising though her treatment was.

She looked around her in the seconds she had left before she was whisked away. Interestingly, it looked a little different from before. She felt like she was in familiar surroundings.

In fact, it looked very much like Rachel's Pool in the mezzanine where she first met the Rescuer. Instead of a darkened cave, she could now make out canyon walls. Memories came back to her of the Rescuer's beautiful face and gentle smile. Was he real? Could such a king exist?

Moments later, the violent whirlpool erupted and started to drag her downwards. She braced herself, thinking, "Here we go again."

"But this can't be what happens," she argued in her mind. "I can't drown in Rachel's Pool. Rachel's Pool is not a place. Rachel's Pool is in my heart. It can't be like this."

She started to laugh as the water sucked her down. "So I can't die here. It's ridiculous. This is my place. There is no way I die in Rachel's Pool. It's filled with the Dunamis. And if you drown in the Dunamis, then you live more powerfully than before." Her heart swelled with joy as she descended. A joy at odds with the situation.

In the dream, she felt like she woke up suddenly, a mist rising off her brain. The vortex released her. It was as though two muscular arms suddenly relinquished their grasp. She popped to the surface like a champagne cork. A deep sea diver resurfacing.

Gasping, she looked around. The darkness had gone. Powdery-red sunlight spilled over everything. Brown and grey cliff walls rose up around her, and there was a gorgeous forest beyond the lip of the pool. A waterfall tumbled down from a great height, coloured wine red, or even blood red, by the mezzanine sun, at the point from which it fell. It splashed water against the rocks and filled the pool with water of a paler hue. She laughed again, feeling totally awake.

"Hello Rachel Race," said a deep and gentle voice. It was the voice of the Rescuer. "How are you?"

Rachel chuckled, feeling lightheaded.

"It is you. I knew it was. You were there, weren't you? In the kitchen. And you're here now, aren't you? It is so good to see you, I can't begin to tell you. How am I? All right I guess, ha ha! But you know that already. I'm okay. But I'm not really okay. But I guess that's okay, because you're with me. And I know how this all ends," she burbled. "So, yeah. I'm okay, I guess!"

The pool was warm like a hot tub. "Oh, Rescuer, what took you so long? Everything's been so horrible."

"I know, Rachel. And I'm sorry you had to go through it."

She kicked about in Rachel's Pool. She loved the way the water caressed her entire body, touching every part of her. It supported her, making her feel weightless, floating on air. This must be what it was like to be an embryo, secure in an amniotic sac. Defenceless but protected. Free of responsibilities. Free from the pressures of life. Safe. Or secured tightly, like a courier package in transit, bubble wrapped, buried in foam packing peanuts. Out of harm's way.

She felt the presence of the Dunamis rise up. It made her body feel electric. Alive. She felt the liberty to dive under the surface. As she did, it was as though her body merged into the water and became part of it. It was like her body was the water itself in Rachel's Pool. She could no longer feel the liquid on her body, it was like the two had become one.

As she resurfaced, she started to hum a tune. She saw that the Rescuer was standing at the side of the stone lip. He looked at her lovingly, with eyes that sparkled. His face shifted from human to preternatural. Translucent. Multi-dimensional. Incredible.

He said, "I did something you will find amusing." His voice was a low-pitched wind chime.

"Tell me."

"The enemy believes you are still lost in the Valenstriuccia's nightmare web."

"Really? So where exactly do they think I am? I can take it. Underwater? Underground?"

"At the moment, they've got you in a bed at Griffton General Hospital."

"How do I die?"

"You don't really want to know."

"No, you're right. Of course, you know my mind, right? Oh, and thank you for pulling me out. But I am curious to know, could you have rescued me earlier?"

"My darling Rachel. For me, nothing is impossible. My greatest desire is to rescue the world, so no one perishes. But the bigger picture is more complex."

"Tell me."

"You know that pain and sorrow and evil exist. The world has many challenges. But I am far greater than evil and brighter than the darkness. You know how even the tiniest light dispels the dark when it fires up in a large room? When you strike a match in the dark it flushes out the gloom in an instant. I am the light of a nuclear flash. My glory shreds the darkness in the fraction of a second. And with that light, hope rushes in like a flood."

Rachel thought for a while and eventually said, "So, why don't you just shred all the darkness, like right now?"

The Rescuer's face became unreadable. Spectral colours washed over it. "I hate the darkness, but I love those caught in it. Even those who hate me. I love them the same as I love those who choose what's right. And I delight in showing mercy."

"Even Samyaza? And those horrible spider monsters?"

"Even them. I must let creation choose, though their works

might be evil. And I must judge rightly. That means evil must ripen and reach its fruition. For there is often light even in the dark ones. To destroy the darkness is to destroy it all. But there is forgiveness for those who turn to me. And if they don't, they must pay the cost. There's no justice where the guilty go unpunished."

"I understand. I think."

"Meanwhile, evil continues, regrettably. It often has its way. For you, this can be very painful. I know. I would spare you if I could. And I do spare you when I can. But I want you to know I do not belittle your suffering, Rachel. And I don't hold it lightly. I know what it is to suffer. And wherever I can, I bring beauty out of pain; celebration out of sorrow. What the enemy means for your harm, I can use for your good."

"Okay," said Rachel. She closed her eyes and enjoyed the warm water. A supernatural peace descended on her. She felt totally relaxed, yielding herself, at a very deep level, to the Rescuer's plan and to his goodness.

When she opened her eyes again, the Rescuer was no longer visible. She laughed, putting her head back into the water. And as she chuckled, his words continued to unpack themselves in her mind, opening up like spring blooms.

Chapter 47

Rory found the climb harder than he expected. The shaft went straight upwards without any reprieve. He scrambled for ages, hand over hand, wedging his fingers and trainers into the slots. Even though people were stronger in the mezzanine world, his body actually felt tired from the exertion. He also had to concentrate hard to avoid falling and this was no fun.

He asked the angel why they couldn't just fly them up one by one. Apparently, this wasn't possible for some reason. Secretly, he thought the angels were being a bit lazy.

So, up they went in single file. Fortunately, once the climb was over he realised it had all been worth the effort. At the top, there was a broad stony plateau lit from end-to-end with glowing angels. It made him gasp out loud when he saw it. There were a hundred of them, waiting there. They illuminated the area, which was long and wide like a mall car park and around ten feet high. A spectacular array of colours mingled together, merging into white where the majority clustered.

Led quietly by Micah, Rory crawled over and joined the others, being one of the last. "Man, we're gonna win," he breathed quietly. Then he listened.

"We are making good progress at the top," one of the angels was saying. Cameron whispered that it was their friend Mattatron speaking.

"Hey, I remember him!"

Mattatron said in a clear voice, "Our scouts tell us this is a massive complex with many floors. Our plan is to invade through the hatch we've created over there. We need to find a way to let the army in at roof level. If we can trap the enemy in the middle, we will increase the likelihood of success. The five are being held prisoner above us. They must be our top priority. Together, they are strong. We need to find them and free them."

"How can we help?" Caleb asked.

"Stay safe. Have faith that we can win. Help us free the prisoners. We will go in first. Follow us, be vigilant and take courage."

"I think we can do that," said Caleb, looking at Daniel. Daniel nodded back with a serious expression.

"Okay, let's go."

Suddenly, fireworks exploded as a hundred angels transformed themselves into lightning bolts and flew through the open hatch at the end of the room. They left behind vibrant streaks of colour: greens, blues, purples, oranges. Each one was represented by a range of different shades.

"Woah," said Rory. "Amazing!"

Only two angels were left behind, the ones who accompanied them through the forest. They were recognisable by their colours. One had his ruby-red sword ready, the other his amethyst purple weapon.

"We will go at your human pace," said the red angel, but not unkindly.

"That's nice of you," said Kumiko. "Not everyone can fly like you guys."

"This time, we can help you ascend," replied the red angel, ignoring her sarcasm.

The angels carefully took them up to the next floor, through the gap in the ceiling. Rory's heart raced as he zoomed upwards, ready to meet whatever was on the other side of the hatch. The ceiling was a thick slab of grey stone, several feet deep. They all passed through without any issues and were deposited gently on the floor.

Once through, Rory saw a long white corridor. Dream Fighter guards were lying on their backs all around the place. Rory assumed they were dead. Daniel checked for him, and confirmed that they were. It made him feel both sad and relieved.

A flash of lime-green light came around the corner and an angel materialised in front of them. He stood tall and announced, "We found the prisoners. This way."

He led them swiftly along the corridor. It was hospital-clean with yellow lights embedded in the ceiling. Rory ran past a series of metal doors. Some of them had been hauled opened by force and were dented heavily, presumably by angelic swords. These rooms were empty.

As they travelled, the angel explained, "We have freed the prisoners but we need you to help them. They are not responsive to us."

They arrived at the occupied cells. In one of them, Rory saw a young girl, pale as death, sitting slumped on a bed. A bulbous spider creature lay bleeding on the floor, thick gunge oozing out of it.

"Yuck. It's one of those things," he cried.

The squishy creature made his stomach turn. It looked dead, and certainly wasn't stirring, he observed. He remembered a big pregnant spider that had fallen on his hand once and made him scream. His dad had taken care of it. Its dead carcass looked like a mini version of this one.

Hearing Rory's comment, Caleb and Serena rushed in to check on him and the girl. "Kids, you can stay out in the corridor," said Serena. "You don't have to see this." It was more of a command than a choice, so Cameron and Rory moved out.

Rory watched them from the doorway. They spoke to the girl gently, trying to rouse her. But like Caleb, Anton and Eli, when they had been attacked by the evil blobs in the caves, she seemed to be stuck in a dream. A nightmare. It would probably take time to bring her out of it, thought Rory. He remembered what

Caleb had been like after his time with these nasty creatures. He shivered.

Next door, Daniel and Arabella found another prisoner. Rory wandered over and peered in. This one was a dark-skinned boy who was pale with fatigue. He was moaning quietly, his eyes staring into space. Like the girl, he was wearing blue tracksuit bottoms, a black shirt and a dark-grey hooded top. He also had a dead creature in his room, over by the opposite wall. There was a long trail of liquid leading from the boy to the monster which lay as still as a rock.

Rory was horrified to see that the prison cells were extremely bare. It was as one might expect, but it didn't make it any less shocking to him. They only had a sink, a toilet, a bed and a shelf. There wasn't even a proper duvet. There was nothing to dry your hands on and nothing to do. No games, nothing. Not even a computer or a TV. It all seemed very cruel to him, keeping them in these conditions. He wondered how he'd cope. It would be very difficult.

Rory quickly learned that the other prisoners were also on this level. There were two more boys, both around the same age. He scampered from room to room, getting a good look at them. Both of them were grey-looking. One seemed to be Spanish or South American and had thick brown hair. Rory liked his dark eyebrows. The other had glasses and was very white. It was hard to tell where he was from, somewhere in Europe perhaps. They were all teenagers, Rory noted. They all looked tired, even though they were asleep.

Suddenly, Lake Emerson shouted from across the corridor, "Hey! I found Rachel!" he hollered. "I think she's okay. She's smiling. But she's asleep. And I can't get her to wake up!"

Chapter 48

Serena stuck her head out into the corridor where Rory was waiting. "I've heard something from the Dunamis. We need to bring them together. They need to be together. Sorry, that's all I've got."

Caleb responded, "Yes, great idea. Everyone, grab a person and carry them to Rachel's cell. We'll figure out what to do afterwards. Kids, stay back, won't you?"

Fortunately, there was no sign of the enemy. The angelic army had made sure of that. This gave them great freedom to move about.

Every so often, an angelic messenger would appear to update them on their progress. They learnt that the Warrior Angels were busy clearing the floor above where there were a lot of armed guards. Rory discovered that the enemy was putting up a tough fight, with casualties on both sides. But the angels had it all in hand and were making good progress. Though he didn't like the idea of angel casualties, he was thrilled at the thought of them beating back the baddies.

In other news, the angels were still working on gaining access to the building from the roof. A messenger explained they had flown up the stairwell and met little resistance. This meant they were able to secure the entire area, all the way up to the roof. They also succeeded in posting guards at all of the doors along the way. Having the element of surprise had worked in their favour on several levels not to mention the roof.

It meant they had completely surprised the enemy above. But it was slow going, gaining ground on the roof. The war was at its fiercest up there. However, the demonic army was now sandwiched between Warrior Angels above and below, the messenger announced. He visually described the scene as being: two thin lines of white with a thick layer of black between them. Rory imagined a burnt steak sandwich on white bread.

In terms of the safety of the group, the angels were able to seal off this basement floor. Guards were posted at the stairs and staircases. So, if the enemy felt like coming down, they would have to smash through a thick layer of armed guards. The messenger said this wasn't going to happen easily.

When it came to shifting the prisoners into Rachel's room, the Harcourt boys were told by several people to stay out of the way. Rory really felt he could have helped though. He was strong and determined, he felt.

The four victims were relatively light for Caleb, Daniel, Micah and Serena to carry, particularly the dark-skinned boy and the oriental girl. They seemed to weigh next to nothing. The other two boys were slightly more muscly, but still no challenge for Caleb or Daniel who were better at lifting than the others.

At the end of their exertions, the nine of them crowded into Rachel's cell and scrutinised the five young people. They were still deeply asleep though Rachel was smiling sweetly.

"She looks just like she did when I found her," said Lake. "Still smiling."

"So, what do we do now? Give them a slapping? Hose them all down?" suggested Kumiko.

Caleb shrugged and looked at Serena. "We have tried to rouse them gently. I guess we just have to wait."

"By the way, I found these by her lap," said Lake, clutching a dozen sheets of handwritten paper.

"What do they say on them?" asked Daniel.

"It's a diary."

Lake said reluctantly, "The first one says 'Rachel's Diary Day 1.' Do you think it's okay to read it? I mean it might be personal."

"Of course it's all right," snapped Kumiko. "She wrote it for a reason. If you don't read it, I will. Anyways, it could help us." Kumiko held her hand out.

"Okay," Lake sighed. But he handed it to Arabella instead.

Rory watched his mother sit on the bed and speed-read the entire manuscript. His dad impatiently tapped her arm as she read, with Lake interjecting questions along the way. In response, Arabella made sure she paused from time to time to deliver a sizeable piece of information. "She got kidnapped in the place you went to, Lake."

"Bhutan, yes, I know. What happened after that? Did they hurt her?"

"They brought her over in some sort of box, presumably on an aeroplane."

"Okay, what else?"

"She's been writing her diary for seven days. She says near the beginning that Samyaza said he will kill her today if she doesn't agree to follow him. At least I assume it's today, going by her timing. And the fact she's still alive."

"That's terrible," said Rory.

"What else does she say, darling?" Daniel asked, looking at her intently.

Arabella continued in clipped tones, scanning through the diary. "She met the other four people who were chosen for their fingers. What Serena says is right. The five have some sort of a strong connection through the Dunamis. They can talk to each other in their minds. And they know how to overpower the enemy. When they are together, they are very strong. They can break lights and open doors. And fight the demons," she said excitedly.

Rory watched Caleb wander over to Rachel, and put his hand on her forehead. Meanwhile, Daniel and Micah tried unsuccessfully to rouse the others again.

Arabella read on, speaking quietly. She was jumping around the diary, picking through. Trying to make sense of Rachel's ordeal.

"Early on, they tried to use Rachel's friend Lara against her. It sounds like Lara's been turned. Oh, this is horrible. They brought Eddie in, in a coffin. To put pressure on her, you know. And Rachel made friends with one of the guards. Samantha. She helped Rachel escape. But the enemy killed her. That only just happened. Yesterday I think."

"This is awful," said Lake. "What they put her through."

"Rachel and the others managed to escape to the roof. The enemy is powerful up there. Like the angels said to us. The five got captured. Samyaza brought in the nightmare creatures. She was conscious when they put one on her head. She still manages to write, though her handwriting is shaky. Then it just stops. That's where her account ends." Arabella looked up suddenly, bird-like.

Unexpectedly, they heard Rachel's voice. "What are you all doing here?" she slurred, making Lake jump.

Rachel sat up against the wall and looked around unhurriedly. "Am I dreaming?"

The other four sat up simultaneously. Ten eyes, that were previously closed, regarded the visitors drowsily.

"Whoa, freaky," said Rory.

Rachel suddenly saw Lake. She smiled sleepily and said in a croaky voice, "Hey stranger. Someone throw a party in my cell? Anyone gonna pour me a drink?"

Lake knelt down and threw his arms around her, then everybody started speaking at once.

Chapter 49

Holding a joint conversation between fourteen people proved very challenging, Rory observed.

At first, Rachel was the natural centre of attention.

"So, you read my diary?" she asked Lake, casually.

"Err, yes. We did. It was on the floor over there," he said sheepishly.

"You read my personal diary," Rachel asked Kumiko, her voice growing harder.

Kumiko shrugged. "Sure."

"My private writings?" She stared angrily at her.

"Yeah. We read your diary, sleeping beauty. Keep your hair on," said Kumiko.

Lake added defensively "We didn't mean to intrude. It was just that we thought It would help us figure out what to do."

"Lake!" shot Rachel, fuming.

"When you guys didn't wake up, I mean."

Rachel burst out laughing. "Oh, you lot are so easy to mess with," she grinned. "You need to lighten up. It's not the end of the world. Well, actually, it might be." She laughed again.

Everyone relaxed. Next, they chatted excitedly about being freed. They shared stories with each other about their terrible dreams. They quickly gathered they were safe for now, guarded by scores of warriors, but that danger lay ahead of them.

Rory noticed the five didn't seem to be suffering any lasting

209

effects from their time under the power of the Valenstriucciae. Not like when Caleb was tortured by them. Or like when he got captured himself, though he didn't remember much about it.

Their minds seemed clear, and they appeared positive, though weary. He recalled how Caleb had been, in comparison. That had been very confusing because he thought so highly of Caleb. After they got him out of the cave, he seemed so hopeless for a long time. Even Daniel and Rachel couldn't snap him out of it.

Rory knew in his heart it wasn't Caleb's lack of trust in the Rescuer, but the enemy's work. The enemy had a way of sapping your energy and your hope. And then Caleb had gone away, flying with an angel. When he came back, he was back to his old self except his hair was white. Like Rachel's or Lake's, and now Kumiko's.

Once the five had finished chatting amongst themselves, there were proper introductions all around. They realised that between the fourteen of them, they covered almost every continent, either through birth or travel: Europe, America, South America, Africa and Asia.

Rory's favourite one of the five was Ndege, and Cameron said he liked Paolo. They told them too, which went down well. Rachel and Jia Li seemed to be instant friends, Rory thought. What was amazing was the Dunamis helped everyone communicate with each other, overcoming any language barriers.

After hearing the stories of the five, Caleb and Serena talked about their Protector. Next, Rory and Cameron got the opportunity to tell everyone about theirs. Then Lake spoke briefly about his Protector and quietly explained about how Eddie's life came to an end. Rachel took this well, Rory thought.

They spent a brief time communing with the Rescuer through the Dunamis, which Rory enjoyed. Particularly the peace that fell over them. When the time finished, Rory felt refreshed. He also noticed the five teenagers looked like they were glowing. It was very strange. And then an angel appeared at the doorway with a surprising request.

"Sons and daughters of mankind. We need your help," said the angel of light.

"Our help? You need our help?" asked José, incredulously.

"We have cleared the way as far as we were able. But we are facing fierce resistance from the Grigori and the Nephilim. They have gathered with Samyaza on the roof and command a large army of Angel Hunters."

"What about the Dream Fighters?" Kumiko enquired. Rachel looked at her, then glanced at her white hair, Rory noticed.

"We have dealt with them," replied the angel.

"All of them?"

"No more Dream Fighters remain in the mezzanine."

"The whole of the mezzanine? I see. So just the others then. The big ones?" said Lake.

"Yes. The big ones, as you say. The Angel Hunters, Grigori and Nephilim. Come quickly. It would be best for the five to come first."

Rachel led the way out of the cell, walking confidently. Rory thought he saw Lake gawping at her with his mouth open. He chuckled.

°°°°°12345°°°°°

Rory breathed a sigh of relief. There were no baddies out in the corridor.

"Hey Cam, what do you reckon?"

"About what?"

"You know, what's waiting for us up there."

"It's hard to tell in this crazy place. I just hope there aren't any more shape shifters."

"Or any more of those blobs," said Rory. "Valenstricken – how do you say it?"

"I'm not sure," Cameron admitted.

They followed Micah and their parents, who walked behind Caleb and Serena, with the five leading the way with the angel.

Behind them were Lake and Kumiko. The hallway eventually brought them to a wide stone staircase. This led up from the basement. As they went, they saw a couple more angels guarding the route.

They halted briefly at the top of the stairs, where one of the angels said, "Be wary of the enemy and have your guard up at all times. They are fast, ruthless and unpredictable."

"Why do you need us? Can't you take care of them yourselves?" queried Lake. "I mean, what can we do? I've seen those monsters up close. You don't want to mess with them. And we don't have any swords!"

"Do you still not understand, son of mankind? We will do the main fighting, but you have the Dunamis in you. Your faith is our fuel. You are powerful. Also, this is your battle, and the war is also between you and the enemy. We must do this together."

"Take heart, young Lake. We can do this," said Caleb. "And whether we live or die, we live in the presence of the Creator. Here or in the life to come."

"Enough messing about. Let's finish this," said Rachel, charging ahead. She paused momentarily. "Which way do we go?"

"Along that corridor. You will find a large chamber. We are using that as a staging post to go up to the next floor," explained an angel.

Moving as one body, the five led the way. Rachel and Jia Li were at the front, striding ahead confidently. The two boys, Ndege and José were close on their heels, with Paolo at the rear. Rory imagined that they were communicating silently with each other all the time. They certainly seemed to know what each other was thinking. It was like they were one person. Perfectly in step. Sometimes, they even turned their heads the same way. It was pretty freaky, Rory felt. But he liked it.

In the next room, an impressive whitewashed hall, angels went up and down through the ceiling. As they flew, they were represented either by coloured flashes of light or a swish of dazzling white clothing. There were a number of sizable holes through which Rory could see thick layers of stone floor. Piles of debris lay at the bottom. Grey mounds of stone that used to be ceiling.

Two tall ladders rested at the mouths of two of the holes. Reaching down and connecting this floor to the next. Rory observed that the ladders weren't like ones you can buy in the shops. These had been assembled from irregular twigs and branches. Soot-black rods of wood from the trees in the mezzanine forest. Woven expertly together using dark twine.

"It's all right. The floor above is clear, and we have almost completed a sweep of the one above that," the group was told. "We are safe from the enemy for the time being. But be on your guard always."

Without delay, they all climbed up a level. Cameron wanted to go up a different ladder from Rory, and the adults let him. He thought this was a bit unfair that Cameron got to use a different ladder all to himself. But he let it go, and they all met up at the top anyway, so it soon got forgotten.

The floor above was altogether darker than the previous one. It was also much broader, a space very like the inside of an airport. It had the same quality of sound as well, Rory thought. Whenever he'd been to an airport, he liked the way the announcements bounced off the walls. Voices echoed around and merged into each other. This place was much the same, and the sounds of their conversation intertwined and wove into the scuffle of footsteps and the rustle of wings.

Both the ceiling and the floor were coal black, embedded with anthracite-grey streaks. The enemy hadn't bothered to paint it and the place smelled musty to Rory.

Looking around, he was horrified to see so many dead Dream Fighters. After all, they were humans like him. In some places they lay in small, leathery heaps. Three or four of them on top of each other. He didn't see any of them moving. They were all lifeless.

Again, flashes of light travelled up to the next floor through gaping holes that had been smashed through the infrastructure. There was only one ladder this time. A wide and stout one. Six angels stood guard at the base of it. They looked stern. Ready to meet any opposition with force.

"What are we to expect above?" Caleb asked.

"Expect anything," was the reply. Rachel started to climb the ladder. She paused halfway, looking back at Jia Li and the others. She nodded. The four of them nodded back in unison. Then she resumed her climb.

Rory watched her disappear through the gap between the floors. He wondered what all the nodding was about but trusted these strange, mystical teenagers. They were all so self-assured, ready for whatever might come their way.

Before anyone else could ascend the ladder, there was a seismic crash. Something punched a car-sized hole through the ceiling ten metres away from them.

Seconds later, a huge chunk of masonry fell heavily to the stone floor beneath. Surfing on top of it were two angry-looking Angel Hunters.

Chapter 50

As the Angel Hunters came into view, a tidal wave of evil rolled towards the group. For an instant, Rory found it hard to breathe. The intruders flew at the group with unexpected force. Spiky black homing missiles. The crowd scrambled, trying to escape. Rory fell backwards onto his bottom, but avoided the enemy. He glimpsed razor-sharp claws and teeth. Dull, soulless eyes, bent on destruction.

One of the demons ploughed straight into Daniel, knocking him off his feet. The other targeted Lake. But Lake leapt into a skater's roll before the point of impact. Meanwhile, Caleb, who was close by, had the presence of mind to kick out hard with his boot. It made the attacker change course and he rushed past like the wind. The monster's momentum carried it far away, towards a distant wall.

Daniel scrambled to his feet, roaring from the back of his throat. Both he and Lake prepared themselves for more. They turned to face the vicious creatures.

Suddenly, Rory saw a stream of Warrior Angels launch themselves at their foe, racing down from above. They made impact. There was a sound of boxing gloves hitting a leather punch bag. A shriek and a hiss. Then, in less than a second, the dark attackers were on the far side of the hall, lying lifeless. The group could breathe again.

Rory's father and Lake were shaken but unhurt. Arabella held

Daniel tightly, and then let him go. Lake brushed himself off in a manly way, and said, "I'm all right. Don't worry about me." If anything, it made them all more determined to press onwards. Take the fight to the enemy.

Ndege poked his head over the hole above. "Everyone okay?" he checked. "Yes? Good to see you are all okay. We had some trouble up here ourselves. But it's over now."

His face disappeared and was replaced by Rachel's. She announced, "Okay? Lake?" He gave her the thumbs up sign.

"Good. All clear here too. You can come up. It's amazing. You'll see."

The next room had a sweeping spiral stairwell at the centre, carved from the same black and grey rock. Fighting angels resolutely guarded the staircase. They were posted all the way up the round construction. Rory thought they were reminiscent of a string of Christmas lights on a tree. At the top, a mass of angels flew around. Like fireflies. A cloud of immense fireflies. Rory smiled, impressed.

Like the previous one, this area was also a voluminous space. Like a mall or an aircraft hangar. Also, the ceiling was much higher than the other floors. It probably made it hard for the angels to build ladders long enough, though anything was possible, thought Rory. Then again, he realised, it did have a massive staircase, so who needs ladders?

He immediately noticed more holes in the ceiling, further along, just like on the floors below. Battle sounds rang out on the floor above. Through the openings he saw the flash of swords, black wings whipping through the air, and dark blood spraying. All of a sudden it hit him. They were about to enter the heart of the battle. Adrenalin flooded his young frame, making him stand up straight.

°°°°°*12345*°°°°°

The landing at the top of the stone stairwell was like the eye of the storm in a hurricane. Rachel stood and looked all around her, trying hard to believe what she was actually seeing with her eyes. And she'd seen a lot of things in the mezzanine.

The dark ceiling was so high it looked like an open sky. You could barely see it, were it not that it was lit so adequately by angel light. Clusters of black-winged, dark-bodied Angel Hunters swarmed everywhere. Fortunately, they raced around high up, with the area directly above being clear. Angels fought continually against them. Every few minutes one or the other would drop out of the air and collide with the ground. A dead angel. A dead demon. It was alarming for the children.

Rachel wondered whether the brothers should be staying below where it was safer. But equally, she knew their presence was as important as the grown-ups'. Everybody had a part to play in the battle.

Rachel checked to see that her people were all right, starting with the four.

"Jia Li, Ndege, José, Paolo?" They were her brothers and sister. The family she never had. Comrades in arms. She loved them dearly.

They quickly checked in with her one by one, their voices sounding in her head.

"We can do this," José commented.

Paolo said, "This is terrifying."

"I love a challenge," said Ndege.

"The enemy is going to pay dearly," Jia Li added.

Satisfied, Rachel glanced quickly at the others. Lake, who didn't make nearly as many bad jokes as he used to. With his floppy hair and dreamy eyes. How she loved him. Next was the wonderfully-transformed Kumiko, whom, she learned, had burned down her house. But, bizarrely, she forgave and held nothing against her. Then there were the wonderful Harcourts, with their lively kids. The family that had turned her towards the Rescuer. And Micah, whom she still found devastatingly handsome but was more of a brother now. Lastly, the Nobles: bold, adventurous Caleb and his gutsy, prophetic wife Serena. She had come to love each and every one of them in a different way.

If these were their last moments on earth together, she would be satisfied. There was no one better to stand alongside and fight. No one better to die alongside. If Lara and Iona were here, that would just be the icing on the cake. And of course her father. She would fight the enemy with everything that was in her for the sake of Eddie and her mother. It was what she was born for.

Only the boys had a hint of alarm in their eyes. The others looked serious but were focusing on one battle or another, willing victory for the angels. Fuelling them with their faith in the Rescuer and his Dunamis.

The battle was truly fierce. But they had the upper hand against their enemies. Fight by fight, skirmish by skirmish, they added their combined efforts, bringing them to an end. Flashes of coloured lightning raced around the cavernous room.

"Those two," Rachel called, pointing upwards. "Bring them together."

The five shone a spotlight in their minds on two big Angel Hunters. They were some distance apart, but were rapidly rounding on a group of Warrior Angels with a fierce intensity, talons at the ready. Superbly, the group flung them through the air, like two beanbags, and sent them hurtling towards each other. Rachel and the others smashed them together, foiling their plot. The Warrior Angels immediately finished off, dashing them to the rocky floor. But there was no time to rest.

"Over there," Rachel told her team, seeing a coordinated onslaught emerging. It involved countless aggressors, travelling at great speed.

"Call on the Dunamis. Ask him to disrupt that attack," she said in her head. Immediately, the five turned towards the descending cloud of shadowy figures. They saw the angel army rocket towards the swarm, swords drawn. Incredibly, they speared every single one of the attacking demons. The creatures plummeted to the ground, screeching.

"Man! Did you see that?" José shouted. "Am I glad I chose the winning side! That's what you get, you worthless bats. That's what you get when you mess with us."

"Focus, José," Jia Li snapped.

But it was too late. An Angel Hunter came out of nowhere. Speeding like a javelin, it sent José flying across the rocks. His body spun like a doll. He eventually came to a stop. Crumpled. Broken. Blood seeped out from under him. It started to form a pool. Meanwhile, three Warrior Angels picked off the attacker. But it was too late. The boy was no longer moving. Rory started to cry.

Chapter 51

"José? José, can you hear me?" Rachel said desperately in her head. Nothing came back.

Paolo shook his head, and Jia Li looked tense.

Caleb ran over to where he lay, accompanied by Daniel. Cradling him in his arms, Caleb looked over and shook his head. He mouthed the word "sorry".

Rachel stared at them. "No," she declared. "This is not how it goes."

She sprinted over to them, bearing down on José. "In the name of the Rescuer, you come back. We need you. I command you to come back to us, José. This fight is not over. We've been through too much together."

But it was fruitless. The Bolivian boy lay limp in Caleb's arms. A crowd of angels flew down to surround them, landing quietly on the pads of their feet, coming to rest. They stood silently, the room now clear of enemy activity. A hush fell over them all, the only noises being distant sounds of battle high above on another level.

"We must bring him back," Rachel shouted.

"Sometimes we are permitted, and sometimes we are not," said Caleb, sadly. "Perhaps this is his time to go."

"I fear he's right, Rachel. Did I ever tell you I saw a boy who looked very much like him?" asked Daniel quietly. "Maybe it was his brother, I don't know. It was in a vision. Looked like

South America to me. Anyway, a cheetah was about to kill him. A demonic creature that looked like a cheetah. It was just like you taught me, Caleb. I asked the Dunamis for mercy, and I believe it saved his life. Although it worked that time, I fear it is too late for this poor boy."

"I can't believe you're standing around telling stories. This can't be how it happens," Rachel said aghast. "How do you know? Caleb, didn't you and Eli bring Daniel back when he fell into the Channel? Off that ferry? You said you pulled him out of the water and he came back to life."

In her head, she said to the other three, who were now with them, "Come on. Help me do this."

As Jia Li, Ndege and Paolo closed their eyes, she turned to give her full attention to José's corpse. He had been dead for many long minutes. Too many perhaps.

Then Rachel declared loudly, "Through the power of the Dunamis, we command you to wake up, José. Wake up right now. You come back to us."

As she stood back, José opened his eyes and gasped for air.

"See? I told you guys. You just have to have faith," she shouted triumphantly.

Caleb and Daniel grinned like little boys.

José's eyes roamed around crazily for a moment. They fell on each face, one at a time, and then searched the room, end-to-end.

Then he said rapidly, "What did I miss? Where have all the flying things gone? Aww, man. I'm bleeding all over you. Sorry, dude."

Jia Li ran over and gave him a hug. Then she punched him in the arm.

"How do you feel?" asked Daniel.

"Feel okay. Back hurts a bit. Did we win?"

"Sorry son. I'm afraid it's not over yet."

"You are correct," said a flash of light that transformed quickly into an angel, having travelled down from above. "This level and several floors above are now clear. We are able to take care of the remaining ones but we need your help on the roof. The Grigori and their Nephilim are gathering with the demon army. They mean to come to us unless we meet them first. There is no time to lose."

Nice pun, dude. Yeah, this is no time to lose," said Lake.

"Right," said Rachel. "Do you feel ready, José?"

"Who me? Yeah, of course I'm ready. I'm always ready. Let's smash those demons in the face."

"That's the spirit," said Caleb.

°°°°°*12345*°°°°°

The angels carried them individually up through the floors. Some of them had experienced travelling like this before on longer journeys, particularly the Harcourts. They had flown from Midway Atoll, in the middle of the ocean, all the way back to Griffton. Caleb had also done his trip with Mattatron the time he met the Rescuer.

Daniel, too, went with the angel Sarakiel to rescue Rory from the mezzanine caves. And Lake had been borne aloft in the mezzanine the time when the ground crumbled beneath him. Nevertheless, it was a thrilling experience for everyone.

Above the chamber that seemed to have no ceiling, there were several layers of more traditional floors. Some of them were painted white. Most were carved from the same black and grey rock as the lower levels. From time to time, they saw clumps of organic matter. Bulbous growths in dark greens and deep purples.

Up they went, through a range of staggered holes, some larger than others. Rachel's angel explained that they had spread the gaps between the opening so the enemy couldn't rush straight down. By being forced to travel horizontally, the Warrior Angels were more likely to hinder and halt attacks.

The strategy had worked well. On each floor, they saw macabre bodies sprawled lazily or piled up. Blood and gore lay around the carcasses. Dream Fighters. Angel Hunters. Valenstriucciae.

There was also an amazing range of monsters they had never seen before. Giant eyeless creatures with grey tentacles. Others with long black spikes, reminiscent of humongous sea urchins. Some had untenably long tendrils. One was made entirely of purple rolls of fat.

Rachel felt relieved she hadn't met any of these and that the angels had dispatched them all. Near the top was another incredibly tall chamber. This was like a large industrial warehouse. There were hundreds of rectangular boxes. Cages perhaps.

Finally, they popped out of the roof, all fourteen of them along with their guardian angels. What Rachel saw there was the most unbelievable scene she had ever encountered.

Chapter 52

The entire angel army was ranged against the forces of darkness and evil before their very eyes. Seemed like it at least. It was intense. Like the biggest New Year's Eve fireworks party. There was nowhere in the sky that was motionless. Violent warfare exploded right across the horizon. Winged beings raced about endlessly at top speed, darting back and forth. Attacking, retreating, stabbing and parrying. Spiralling upwards and swooping back down like broad-winged birds of prey: bald eagles, hunting kestrels, racing hawks. Made of either luminescent light or the very darkness itself.

"Unbelievable," said Lake, and then fell into contemplative silence. The place where they were deposited was guarded heavily by a garrison of Warrior Angels. It formed a protective area around them. The air above was occupied by hovering fighters. Beyond them was another layer of protectors.

They stood on a massive rooftop almost without end. The edge was just about visible in the remote distance. Beyond the top of the citadel was a circle of black mountains. It was like they stood on a lone island in a sea of jagged peaks.

Rachel immediately fell into the role she'd been born for. Connecting with the minds of the others, she said, "Let's give these angels some backup."

The others assented right away.

"Let's begin over there," said Jia Li. "We need to disrupt them."

She pointed to a thick mist of Angel Hunters. They raged around, nipping at the lines of Warrior Angels. One or two fell from the sky from time to time, leaving behind streaks of light.

The five applied themselves to the task. They found immediate success calling on the Dunamis to overpower the enemy. Very soon, they watched scores of them fall into the depths like huge black raindrops. Encouraged, they worked even harder to turn the battle in favour of their fighters. Meanwhile, the others entreated the Dunamis to favour the Warrior Angels. They witnessed victories all around, from one end of the sky to the other.

Buoyed by their achievements, the group showed little concern when the Grigori and the Nephilim appeared at the edge of the roof. They landed like great vultures, carried on immense wings. Massive angels of darkness, like their brother Samyaza, they roared, suddenly striking terror in the hearts of the group as they announced their presence.

There were around a dozen of them, with a similar number of Nephilim offspring. The latter were both beautiful and hideous. Their faces and bodies comprised the beauty of human creatures, but were horribly distorted by the fallen nature of their demonic parents.

"Quick. We need to shift our focus," Rachel signalled to the others. Their angelic protectors immediately sprung into action. A hundred of them propelled themselves at the new arrivals, like so many coloured flares. They created a wave of light, flowing outwards towards the edge of the roof. Some of these homing missiles hit their marks. Others were batted away by the overwhelming force of their aggressive targets. But they came back just as strongly like angry wasps claiming their revenge. Many Warrior Angels were extinguished, however. Summarily ejected from the mezzanine.

The Grigori and their Nephilim were relentless in reaching the group of humans. Their deafening bays filled the air. Nothing was going to stop them. They were coming for blood, hatred in their eyes.

"Go for one of them. The big one in the middle," Rachel commanded her friends. They joined forces to wield as much power as they could at one of the fallen angels. Incredibly, the Rescuer gave them instant victory over him. With an explosion that sounded like a sonic boom, they blasted him backwards and he accelerated off the edge of the roof. The boys cheered with delight.

"Keep going," said Rachel. "Let's try one of those ugly ones. Far left."

They also threw him violently backwards. An eager troupe of Warrior Angels cut him down.

"Good strategy. Same again only faster," Rachel commanded.

She directed them down the line as quickly as they could go, picking off their foe and empowering the flying army to finish the job. In the sky above, the Warrior Angels were winning at last. There was more light than darkness up there now, from the centre to the remote recesses. A kaleidoscope of dense colours swirled around endlessly, flecked with black specks. Behind it, a lilac and magenta mezzanine sky could be seen.

Back on the roof, Rachel and her team found some creatures harder than others to conquer. But, one by one, the enemy eventually fell. Sometimes they took many angels with them, raging and clawing as they went. Sometimes they departed quickly, spiralling off the side.

And then it was over. The sounds of fighting died down as battalions of angels searched the skies for any remaining enemies. Signs of carnage were evident all over the place. Dead demons littered the roof. Two Nephilim lay motionless fifty metres away the size of two dead gorillas. Their reign of terror had come to an end.

The five embraced each other, tears in their eyes. The others exchanged hugs all around. But as the Harcourts checked on each other, Arabella said, with panic in her voice, "Where's Rory? Has anyone seen him?"

"And where's Lake?" asked Rachel, glancing about.

Kumiko added, "What a time to go walkabouts!"

They looked around, desperate to locate the missing pair. The angels didn't seem to know, and nobody could see them on the roof.

They found out soon enough. Out of one of the outlying holes in the roof, the furthest away from them, emerged a creature. It was the repellent and fast-moving figure of Samyaza. His skull-like face grinned but without any humour. He was clutching Lake under one arm and Rory under the other.

"Stay back," he commanded menacingly. He rose above them, keeping his distance from the Warrior Angels who were itching to stop him in his tracks. Rory screamed loudly and continually. Lake tried to wriggle and punch, but his movement was severely restricted.

Chapter 53

"I am so very tired," said Samyaza theatrically. "And when I get tired, I'm prone to drop things. Or hug them too tightly, if you know what I mean. Ah, hello Daniel. Nice house you've got. I particularly enjoyed your taste in Jacobean dark-wood furniture. And that study of yours. Just superb. We could have done great things together you know. You and I. And my little Kumi," he spat.

"I thought you loved me. Still hanging onto your wretched little life, I see. How quickly you switched your affections. You disgust me. And Rachel. Dearest Rachel. Look what you've become. You're so smug. So confident. But, at the end of the day, you're just the Rescuer's puppet. On your own, you amount to exactly nothing. A lonely little zero. You make me vomit," he said with intense hatred in his voice.

Samyaza continued, "Caleb oh so Noble. You are a thorn in my flesh. You're no better than her. I won't even waste my breath on you. And of course, the rest of the famous five. All my favourites are here. José, you never would have made it as a Dream Fighter. Too soft." He rose above them, staring with disdain at the crowd. Rory widened his eyes. Lake kicked out in vain. But he stopped as soon as Samyaza lifted up his bony hand and scratched it across Lake's cheek, making him bleed. He yelped in pain. "There, there," said Samyaza, mockingly.

"Should we take him?" Rachel asked the others in her head.

"I don't know. He's fast," replied Ndege.

"And he might drop the others," said Paolo.

"At least we should try," Jia Li reasoned.

"José? What do you think? Are you ready?" asked Rachel.

Suddenly, Cameron shouted, "You're a bully. Let my brother go."

"Hold on a sec," Rachel told the others. "I don't want him to kill Rory. By accident or on purpose. Or Lake either." She saw that Daniel was tight-lipped and Arabella was fighting back the tears.

"This isn't about them, is it?" shouted Rachel. "Put them down. You don't want to harm them."

"That's where you're wrong." Samyaza stabbed his long talons into Lake's shoulder, piercing his flesh through to the bone. Lake let out a blood-curdling scream.

"Stop! Stop that! It's me, isn't it? It's always been about me."

"We could have ruled the world, Rachel," roared the dark angel. "I chose you. It was always you. If only you had it in you to love me like you love him. Worship me like you worship him. This would all be so different."

"Never!" She hollered.

At that, Samyaza unexpectedly pitched Rory at the ground. The terrified child didn't have time to shout as he raced downwards. Seconds before impact, a Warrior Angel swooped down and rescued him, ferrying him to safety. He landed far away and stood tall over the boy.

Samyaza shrugged, still holding onto Lake. "It's day seven, Rachel. I might as well ask the question one last time. Are you ready to follow me? By the way, the answer is yes. And if it isn't, I'm going to crack this one's head open like a nut, right in front of you. Your choice."

"Get ready for action," Rachel said privately to the five. "We need to stop him right now. Follow my lead."

And to the beast she said, "Samyaza. Look at my hair. What does it tell you?"

Samyaza hovered up and down slowly on his broad black wings.

"It tells me, you won't join me. And you love the Rescuer. But are you ready to die for him?"

"Yes I am."

"Well, seven days is up Rachel. It's time for you to die."

Samyaza suddenly threw Lake with unexpected force at the place where Daniel was standing. As he hurtled towards Daniel and the hard roof, a dozen angels swooped down, coordinating their rescue. They swiftly lifted Lake out of harm's way. But it was of no concern to Samyaza who had merely used it as a distraction.

He flew directly at Rachel like a bullet from a gun. Talons first, he bore down on her: a streak of black lightning. The demon lord moved with supernatural speed, barely leaving any time for his foes to react. Except for Kumiko.

She physically threw herself in front of Rachel and took the full impact of the dark angel's flight. The group looked on in horror as Samyaza speared Kumiko with his bony fingers, reaching through her body to impale Rachel as well.

Kumiko screamed in pain momentarily as she died. At the same time, Rachel felt the sharp spikes tear into her. She knew her time was also up.

"Now my friends. Now is the time," were her last instructions to the five. Together, Rachel and the others called on the Dunamis to destroy Samyaza once and for all. Seconds later, it was done.

Unseen, the Rescuer looked on, sad that his enemy had finally met his doom. Sorrowful about the choices Samyaza had made. He took no pleasure in any of it.

As Rachel smiled, and then collapsed, the Rescuer caught her in his arms and brought her through death and into the light.

"It's time to go home," he said.

Chapter 54

Statues of Samyaza were crumbling all across the world. Massive wings dropped to the ground and smashed to pieces on the high hills and urban summits over which they had presided so proudly. Warrior Angels, borne aloft by the Rescuer's faithful followers and the three Protectors, pursued and eradicated the Dream Fighters, Angel Hunters and the remaining Grigori and Nephilim wherever they skulked on the earth. A new day had arrived.

The Rescuer gave his people a new instruction. They were to find an enemy of the King and heartily embrace them. Tell them about the Rescuer. Heal their bodies and their hearts. Show them love.

"Tell them you love them and urge them to turn from their evil ways and trust the true King, the Rescuer," he told them in a simultaneous broadcast across the planet. One that played on the big screen of their minds.

He continued, "The Protectors will assist you. You will face resistance. Many of you will be killed and you and I will meet face to face. But many people will turn. And as that happens, a new dawn will come because I love you and I'm making everything new."

So, all across the earth, Rescuer followers in hiding approached their former enemies. Millions of lights blazed and then went out across the globe as brave individuals were met with a violent end.

But even more succeeded.

Ben and Iona sat on Griffton Cliff holding hands and looking out across the city. The tall buildings were still shrouded in darkness, suffering without electricity. But in the distance, they could see the water rippling under a dark indigo sky, crammed with stars.

The two of them watched the lights winking across the valley here and there. Not a great number, but bright enough to discern amidst the darkness.

Iona gazed at Ben and smiled. "Hey handsome. Let's go find someone to hug," she said. He nodded and allowed her to pull him up. They wandered off together to find out if there was anyone left in the field where the stone statue used to stand.

°°°°°5fingers°°°°°

Also by Joshua Raven

5fingers: initiation - descent into darkness
5fingers: vortex - the mysterious arrival
5fingers: trinity - cut from fire
5fingers: rescue - The Three Protectors

Follow Joshua Raven's blog at www.joshuaraven.com
Instagram: @RavenWrites
Twitter: @RavenWrites
Facebook: Joshua Raven Author
Pinterest: Joshua Raven 5fingers

ABOUT THE AUTHOR

Joshua Raven lives in the South of England with his wife and three children.

He has enjoyed twenty five years as an international journalist and editor, interviewing leading figures in business and technology, and writing for publications and businesses across the globe.

Joshua blogs at www.joshuaraven.com and Tweets/Instagrams at @RavenWrites

5fingers: initiation – descent into darkness

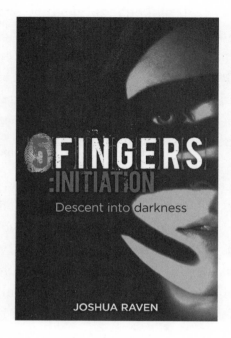

5fingers book one

5fingers: initiation is the first in a five-book series for adult/ teen readers. This supernatural thriller has a cliff hanger in every chapter and lots of surprises.

In 5fingers: initiation, sixteen-year-old loner, Rachel Race, is hurled into a world of darkness and intrigue and forced to carry out a series of assignments by an enemy with many faces.

Rachel teams up with trainee reporter Lake Emerson to solve a mystery of epic proportions.

Paperback, eBook and audiobook available from www.5fingers.co.uk
ISBN: 978-0-9557594-0-6

5fingers: vortex – the mysterious arrival

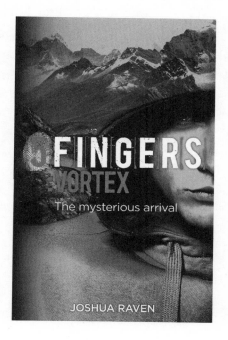

5fingers book two

A year on, the dramatic events of 5fingers: initiation are beginning to recede from Rachel Race's mind. But with her friends scattered and her enemies thirsty for revenge, Rachel and Lake are on for the adventure of their lives.

In 5fingers: vortex the mystery deepens as the darkest minds on earth activate their master plan.

The story follows on from 5fingers: initiation, but can be read standalone.

Paperback and eBook available from www.5fingers.co.uk
ISBN: 978-0-9557594-1-3

5fingers: trinity – cut from fire

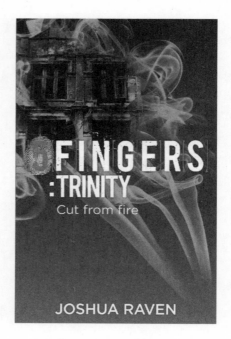

5fingers book three

In the third book of this five-book series, Rachel Race, the heroine, finds herself alone in a land of beauty and horror, where angels and demons tread.

Along with a life-changing encounter that will prepare her for a showdown with evil incarnate, Rachel embarks on the adventure of her life. The ebb and flow of its intensity will carry you through the pages to its dramatic conclusion and leave you wanting more.

The story follows on from 5fingers: vortex, but can be read standalone.

Paperback and eBook available from www.5fingers.co.uk
ISBN: 978-0-9557594-4-4

5fingers: rescue – The Three Protectors

5fingers book four

In 5fingers: rescue, the 4th book in the quintet, hideous beings turn the Earth into their playground: creating havoc wherever their shadow falls.

The world has changed forever. Samyaza is on the loose. Scarred by her encounter with the Malkin, Rachel Race sets out to turn back the tide of darkness. By her side: fearless Caleb, level-headed Daniel; and reporter Lake Emerson, back from his betrayal with Kumiko.

As in initiation, vortex and trinity, the Angel Hunters and Warrior Angels battle it out in the mezzanine world where anything can happen. Nowhere is safe.

Paperback and eBook available from www.5fingers.co.uk
ISBN: 978-0-9934011-0-7